"This is killing me, Cricket," he whispered

He put his other hand to her cheek, cupping her face in both hands now.

"You mean the you-know?" she asked.

"Yes," Tucker said, tilting his head. "We can't do this." He moved in.

"No, we can't," she said, standing on her toes, tipping up her mouth. It was as if some terrific force field pulled them together.

"This would be bad."

"I know," she said, moving closer. "Very bad." As desperate as she was for his mouth, for that hot, dissolving feeling, she would not be the one who kissed first. She couldn't be. He was married. Unhappily, according to his wife, but still. He had to be the one to make the first move.

He wouldn't do it, she saw.

But she definitely would. With that thought, she grabbed his face and pulled his lips to hers.

Dear Reader,

Cricket and Tucker's story is dear to me because it's set in a school. As a former teacher, I felt as though I was living and breathing Copper Corners High on every page I wrote. I even started to have teacher anxiety dreams—you know, where it's the end of the year and you realize you've forgotten to teach reading to your second graders? Needless to say, I related to Cricket's idealism and her insecurity about teaching, which is a very difficult job.

What I love about Cricket and Tucker is how much they want to do the right thing, even when they are doing it all wrong. Ever been there? Had good intentions, but fouled up anyway? For these two, the issue is being honest with themselves about who they are and what they really want. They have so much heart and so much passion for each other and their work. Just thinking about them makes me sigh. These two really got to me. I hold their story close to my heart. I hope they get to you, too.

I'd love to hear from you! Write me at dawn@dawnatkins.com. For news of upcoming books, please drop by my Web site, www.dawnatkins.com.

My very best to you,

Dawn Atkins

Books by Dawn Atkins

HARLEQUIN TEMPTATION
871—THE COWBOY FLING
895—LIPSTICK ON HIS COLLAR
945—ROOM...BUT NOT BORED!

HARLEQUIN BLAZE
93—FRIENDLY PERSUASION

HARLEQUIN DUETS
77—ANCHOR THAT MAN!
91—WEDDING FOR ONE/
   TATTOO FOR TWO

HARLEQUIN FLIPSIDE
11—A PERFECT LIFE?

DAWN ATKINS

WILDE FOR YOU

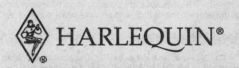

HARLEQUIN®

TORONTO • NEW YORK • LONDON
AMSTERDAM • PARIS • SYDNEY • HAMBURG
STOCKHOLM • ATHENS • TOKYO • MILAN • MADRID
PRAGUE • WARSAW • BUDAPEST • AUCKLAND

To the dedicated teachers of Arizona, who daily make a difference. You humble me.

Acknowledgments

I wish to thank Jenn MacColl, whose rain-forest classroom inspired me to write Cricket's story. Jenn, an accomplished teacher, shares Cricket's absolute commitment to her students. Jenn, my son and I thank you. I also want to thank all the teachers in my life—past and present. You do indeed touch the future. The endangered-owl controversy in this book is fictional, although pygmy owls are, in fact, endangered and live only in southern Arizona and northern Mexico.

ISBN 0-373-69190-4

WILDE FOR YOU

1

IF HE GOT THE JOB, he'd forget women, Tucker Manning vowed, soaping up in the shower. He would be absolutely dedicated. Completely committed. No distractions. No hobbies. No sidetracks.

And no women.

He scrubbed his face, then shoved it under the spray to rinse. Steam rose around him, hot as his conviction.

He needed this job—assistant principal at Copper Corners High—if he was ever to get the one he'd lost.

Lost because of a moment of insanity with a woman who reminded him of someone he couldn't forget. A moment witnessed by three members of the freshman girls' volleyball team, who'd stumbled on him and Melissa in the equipment room...on the vault bench...working out...of their clothes.

Who knew the girls practiced so late?

So, if he got this job, no more women. He scrubbed between his toes, hot water peppering his back, the shower air lush and thick as a jungle.

"Tuuuuck-er, I'm lonely," Julie, the woman he'd been seeing for the last month, called to him. He sighed, letting the water sluice down his body. Okay, maybe one more woman. Except she lived here—

Phoenix—over two hours away from Copper Corners, which was barely a cactus clump off the highway south of Tucson. If he was truly dedicated, he'd have no time for road trips. Or Julie.

He'd stay nose to the grindstone. Just for the two or three years he had to wait for another chance at the position at Western Sun High, when the guy who'd gotten the job retired.

He needed that time to prove to Ben Alton, the principal and his friend, that he had what it took to be a good administrator. An administrator who knew how to keep his head on straight…and his zipper zipped.

The turndown still stung. Tucker hated to lose, but, worse, he'd let Ben down—disappointed the man who'd turned him around back when Tuck was in high school.

The whole reason Tucker had come back to Western Sun with his English degree from the University of Arizona was to work for Ben, who'd become the principal and been given the difficult task of guiding the school through the growing pains that came with a changing neighborhood. Once on the faculty, Tucker had started on his administrator credential, so he could work side by side with his mentor.

For the three years he'd been at Western Sun, he'd been busy—volunteering for curriculum committees, serving as English department chair and as a union rep—and he was liked by students and faculty alike.

But at the end of the interview for the vice principal job, Ben had told him no. *Your heart's in the right place, Tuck. Folks like you, but they don't think you take the work seriously. You're young.*

He'd been stunned. He'd argued—pointed out all he'd accomplished and that age was irrelevant to talent—until the truth had dawned on him that it was the thing with Melissa.

That didn't help, Ben had admitted. *And I'd be playing favorites to hire you in spite of it.*

Tuck had assured him it was a one-time occurrence, despite the gossip. *I have not, quote, been with every female I could get into an empty closet. Melissa was special...and I was just...we were only...okay, it was a bad idea, but it was after hours and we had our clothes on.*

Though belts and zippers had been in motion when the three volleyballers bounded into the room to gape and gasp at Tucker and Melissa putting the horse vault bench to uses for which it was never intended.

The one good thing was that Melissa had been more amused than embarrassed by the incident, for which he'd taken full responsibility.

Tuck understood Ben's decision, disappointed though he was. The top job for an assistant principal was student discipline, so being respected was crucial. The make-out incident had made him the butt of too many jokes for much respect to remain.

Ben had put in a good word for him with Harvey Winfield, the principal at Copper Corners High—a friend of a friend from Ben's Ph.D. program. A small school would be great experience, Ben claimed, since the principal and the assistant shared most duties, instead of having distinct tasks like at Western Sun, where Ben had two assistants, each with different responsibilities.

After Tuck had a few good years at Copper Corners, some accomplishments and professional maturity to tout, Ben would feel comfortable hiring him. And Tucker wanted that. Bad. Because of Ben, of course. And because he'd be damned if he'd be chased out by one mistake and the rumor mill. He'd be back. No question.

And the road back ran straight through Copper Corners, Arizona.

Tucker ran the scrubber over his back, then turned to take in a mouthful of water to gargle and spit.

The interview had gone well, and he'd liked Harvey, who reminded him of his own grandfather—quiet and old-fashioned. Gruff, but with a big heart.

He leaned forward, fingers flat on the black-and-white checkered tile, water falling over his head and neck, and remembered Ben's final comment. *If you get the job, behave yourself*, he'd said, as if Tuck were an errant child. *There are no secrets in a small town. You buy a pack of condoms and everyone will know whether they're ribbed or smooth.*

That wasn't fair. The incident with Melissa had been unusual. She'd reminded him of a girl he'd had a major thing for in college—Cricket. Cricket what? He didn't even know her last name. She'd been Sylvia's roommate. One night senior year, right before Christmas break, while he'd waited for Sylvia to show up at her apartment, he and Cricket had shared a beer, an intense conversation and, once it became clear Sylvia had stood him up, the hottest make-out session he'd experienced. Ever, now that he thought about it.

Melissa had the same kind of fire and attitude as Cricket. She kind of smelled like her, too—sweet and spicy and all woman—and when she came on to him after a curriculum meeting, he'd lost his head. And, as a result, the job he was meant for.

He'd known better, too. He'd been wild in high school and from time to time fought the urge to just blow off responsibility, go with his impulses and play 24/7. Maybe that had shown in his work at Western Sun. He'd had fun with his students, but that didn't mean he didn't take teaching seriously. Worse, he had the uncomfortable sense that Ben was among those who thought he wasn't serious enough to be a good administrator.

They had him wrong, dammit, Tuck thought, smearing green shampoo into his hair and scrubbing hard. And twenty-six was plenty old enough to know what mattered.

If he got the Copper Corners job, he'd watch his every step. The best way to handle temptation was to avoid it, and he was sure Copper Corners would offer few distractions. Rural towns had trouble attracting teachers anyway, and young, single people gravitated to cities for the social life.

He scrubbed his hair, wondering if Harvey Winfield had liked him as much as he'd seemed to. There were other candidates for the job, he knew, but they couldn't possibly want it as much as Tuck did.

"Tucker!" Julie yelled from the bedroom.

He tipped his head back and shouted upward, "I'll be right out."

Seconds later, though, the shower door opened and a naked Julie held one hand over the mouthpiece of the phone. God, she was gorgeous. He'd pull her into the water for a wet adventure after this call....

"It's the principal at that school," she whispered, grinning. "I told him how excited you were about the job."

He took the phone. "Harvey?" he said, hopping out of the stall to clutch a towel to his groin. The man couldn't see through the phone, but Tuck felt damned unprofessional standing there naked. "Good to hear from—"

The shampoo-slick phone slipped out of his hand and hit the floor. Julie bent for it and thrust it at him in time for him to hear Harvey say, "...but after speaking to Julie just now, I've decided to go with my instincts."

"What was that?" he said. "I dropped the phone."

"What I said was that I called to ask a few follow-up questions in case my top candidates declined, but after speaking to Julie I changed my mind. Will you take the job, Tucker? I have a good feeling about you."

"I'd be honored," he said quickly.

Julie gave him a thumbs-up and did a silent happy dance, naked and gorgeous, then mouthed, "Breakfast," and bounced out of the room.

He'd gotten the job. Thank God. Except he hadn't been first choice. Not until Julie said something that changed Harvey's mind. What the hell had she said?

"I'm glad to hear that, Tucker," Harvey said. "I had two fellows with more experience in line—both with excellent references and both from small towns, which is a definite advantage. But knowing that you're married—and to such a supportive woman—I felt comfortable going with my gut reaction...which was to hire you. You're hungry. You're smart. You're serious."

"Knowing that I'm...what?" At that moment, a blob of shampoo dropped into Tucker's eye. Blinking against the sting, he braced the phone with his shoulder and wiped at the shampoo with his hand, but that made it burn worse.

"It's not kosher to ask in the interview, of course," Harvey was saying while Tucker lunged for the sink. The man thought Julie was his wife? How had that happened? Julie had answered the phone at seven-thirty in the morning, for one thing, and raved about him, so of course Harvey had assumed...

"Sure," Tucker said, splashing water into his eye, "but I'm afraid Julie isn't—" The phone slipped out of his fingers again. He grabbed it up, his eyes still burning, in time to hear Harvey say, "—just so very important, Tucker. My last assistant—a single guy— was more interested in the Tucson nightlife than in school business. So it just didn't work out."

"I can understand that," he said, fumbling for a towel, one eye closed, "but, you see, I'm not really—"

Married. I'm not married. That was what he intended to say, except his heel skidded on wet tile and he hit the floor with a smack, the butt pain much worse than the eye burn.

"Tucker? You there?" Harvey said. "What were you saying?"

"I'm here. Just lost my balance." And all sense of reality. "I was saying that I'm not really...."

Through his pain, a vital fact came into his mind: Harvey had better candidates. Two of them. Both more experienced, both from small towns, both married. And politically correct or not, Harvey wanted a married assistant. Being married to a supportive wife was what had gotten Tuck the job offer.

"It's that I'm not..." Tucker had to say something about being a dedicated single guy, but the specter of the Melissa incident rose in his mind. Would Harvey think he was a player? Women hopping in and out of his bed all the time? He wanted to start out on the right foot. This wasn't the way.

"...sure about the housing situation," he heard himself finish, buying time.

"Plenty of rental homes, Tucker. Bring Julie down this weekend and you can find something. I know you see yourself back in Phoenix eventually, but our little town is pretty special. Great place to raise a family, too."

Every second that passed without Tucker correcting the mistake made things worse, he knew, but Harvey was on a roll. "Around here, neighbors help each other. And get in each other's business, of course, but that's two sides of a valuable coin."

The connection went dead for a second.

"There's that damnable click," Harvey said. "This call-waiting business my wife got us into is quite the annoyance. I'd better see who it is. Put the back-to-school faculty potluck on your calendar. In the gym on the first, 6:30 p.m. Looking forward to meeting Julie."

"Thanks, Harvey, but I—"

"Welcome on board, Tucker." And he hung up.

Tuck turned off his phone and sat there on the floor, his back against the tile, his butt aching, his eye running with tears. Now what?

"LET ME GET THIS straight," Tuck's sister-in-law Anna said to him that evening. "You told the principal you were married?"

"No. He assumed it when Julie answered the phone and told him how excited I was about the job. She was trying to be helpful."

Tucker had tried to call Harvey back, as soon as he'd gotten off the floor and tracked down the Winfield number, but had only been connected to voice mail. For hours. He wasn't about to leave an "April fool! I'm not really married" message on the answering machine. In the meantime, he wanted his brother and sister-in-law's take on what had happened. Plus, he needed a dose of his three-year-old nephews, Steven and Stewart, who never failed to cheer him up.

"We're buck nek-ked," Steven chortled, jumping off the ottoman. The boys were fresh from their bath and, in theory, headed for bed.

"Get over here, you slippery seal," Anna said, lunging at Steven. She held Stewart by one arm. "Grab him, Forest."

"You're mine, bucko," Tuck's brother Forest scooped up the bath-pink elf who was older than his twin by ten minutes. Tuck loved the hurly-burly at Forest and Anna's. He loved roughhousing with his nephews, and in a minute, he'd get the privilege of reading them their bedtime story.

With Stewart in a football hold, Anna plopped onto the sofa beside Tuck. "So, why didn't you correct him?"

"I tried, but he kept talking. I'd fallen on my ass and was in pain with shampoo in my eyes. Hell, he offered me the job because he thought I was married.

I was trying to figure out what to say when he had to take a call and hung up."

"So, call him back," Anna said, managing to get Stewart's squirming leg into one side of his pajama bottoms.

"I tried. Voice mail. Now I'll sound like an idiot. 'Oh, gee, I forgot I wasn't married.'"

"Tell him that when you fell, you hit your head and got temporary amnesia, but now you remember that you're actually a babe hound."

"I'm no babe hound."

"What's the big deal about being married anyway? He better not discriminate against single people. That's an EEOC violation if I ever heard one."

"He's worried that a single guy would be bored in Copper Corners. The assistant before me spent too much time chasing women, I guess. Winfield wants someone who'll focus on work, not women."

"How 'bout both? Isn't that your specialty? Having sex *at* work. Much more efficient."

He groaned. He regretted telling Anna and Forest about the Melissa incident more every time Anna brought it up, which was every time he came over, which was often. He loved his sister-in-law, but she was mouthy and opinionated and bossy as hell. His brother worshiped her, though, and that was what mattered.

"I even asked Julie if she'd consider a trip to Vegas…you know, take in a show, do some gambling, swing by a wedding chapel."

Anna stopped, leaving Stewart covered by his pajama top like a superhero-decorated ghost. "You're serious about Julie?" She blinked at him, mouth open, visions of wedding plans glowing in her eyes.

"No. I was joking, though it panicked the hell out of her and now we're pretty much over with."

Anna sighed. "I knew it. You'll never settle down."

"Where's Stewart? Where can he be?" Stewart's muffled voice came from beneath his clothes.

Anna tugged downward on her son's shirt so his head popped out.

"Peekaboo!" he shrieked.

"Peekaboo, sweetie," she said halfheartedly.

"Sure I will," Tuck insisted. "When I'm ready."

"When the moon is blue and my aunt's an acrobat."

"When I find the right woman."

"You wouldn't know the right woman if she had your name tattooed in a heart on her butt."

"You said *butt*, Mommy. Umm."

"Special occasion," Anna said.

Forest leaned down to drop his damp cargo next to Anna to be dressed. "Don't be so hard on him, Anna. Women as great as you don't grow on trees." Forest kissed his wife and their eyes met with warmth.

They were good together. They'd married young—nineteen—and Tuck had feared Forest was scrambling to find something stable after their parents' divorce, but Anna turned out to be perfect for him. In fact, Tucker hoped one day to have the kind of relationship Forest had with his wife—an easy affection, mutual respect and lots of laughter, all built on a bedrock of love.

Except Tucker wanted a woman more like himself than Anna was like Forest. Someone more cooperative, more of a partner, who wouldn't argue every issue into the ground like Anna did with Forest.

Once he was back in Phoenix and got his career on track at Western Sun, Tucker would look for someone. He'd be ready then.

"So, now what are you going to do?" Anna said to Tuck. "Tell the principal that you got a divorce?"

"Tell him it was a mistake, I guess. But why would I lie like that? I'll seem creepy, crazy or lame."

"What you need is a substitute wife," Forest said, putting the freshly dressed Stewart on his shoulders and galloping around the sofa while Stewart shrieked with laughter.

"Sure. I'll just call 'Rent-a-Wife.'"

"You can't afford that," Forest said, lowering Stewart onto the sofa and lifting Steven up for his turn. "Hookers are pricey and housekeepers have skills. Maybe get one of those inflatable women. Prop her in a chair, backlight her and throw your voice like Norman Bates in *Psycho*."

"That's grotesque," Anna said. "And don't get the boys so riled up before bed."

Forest shortened Steven's turn and lowered him to the floor. "Go get books for Uncle Tuck," he said. The twins scampered off, squealing.

"On the other hand, I could say my wife is away taking care of a sick relative…in Australia maybe?" Tucker said.

"Or she could have a job where she travels a lot," Anna mused. "Like in sales. Or maybe with the airlines."

"A stewardess?" Forest asked, sitting beside Anna. "That'd be hot."

"That's flight attendant, not stewardess, you sexist pig," Anna said. "And let's make her a pilot. More impressive."

"That could work—faking a wife, I mean," Forest said. "Hey, you could borrow my old wedding band."

"Your *old* wedding band?"

"We thought he lost it down the sink," Anna said, elbowing her husband, who grimaced in pretend pain. "So we bought a new one. Then I found it behind the bathroom sink faucet. If Mr. Fidget here wouldn't take off his ring every time he washes his hands."

"You want me to get a rash? I don't need a ring to feel married," he said, kissing her cheek. "I'm yours forever."

"Read to us, Unca Tuck! Read to us!" Steven shouted, dragging a book bigger than he was along the carpet. Stewart hopped beside him—a one-man cheering squad.

"Go play for a few minutes, guys," Anna said. "Your mommy and daddy have to straighten Uncle Tuck out."

"Uh-oh," Stewart said, staring at Tuck with round eyes. "Were you berry bad?"

"Kinda bad," he said.

"You have to make good chooses, Unca Tuck," he said somberly. After a sympathetic once-over, the boys turned and galloped off, happy with the extra playtime.

"So, you think I can fake a wife? Except I told Harvey she'd be at the opening-of-school potluck."

"So get someone to stand in," Anna said. "You pissed Julie off, but maybe someone else?"

"Someone else named Julie?"

"Or someone who'd pretend to be her…" Forest said slowly. "I've got it." He leaned across the couch to pick up a framed photo from the end table and turned it toward them. It was a shot of Tucker with his arm around Anna on the terrace of the Del Coronado near San Diego, where they'd all gone for vacation last year.

"You'd be perfect," Forest said to Anna. "You know Tuck and you want the best for him."

"No," Tucker said. "That would be crazy."

"Not necessarily," Anna said. "I could go to the potluck and impress everyone."

"Too much of an imposition," Tucker said, trying to head her off. "You live miles away. There will be more than a potluck to attend, I'm sure."

"But if I were a pilot, I'd have the excuse of working out of town a lot." She tapped her finger on her lip, looking Tuck over. "You want to make a good impression, don't you? You don't want to sound like an idiot or a letch, right? Or like you're hiding a sordid past?"

"Of course not."

"Because that's how you'll sound if you tell the truth now."

"But still…"

"And you can pay us back baby-sitting the twins while Forest and I go away for a weekend or two."

"Thanks for the offer, Anna, but it's too complicated."

"You don't think I can do it, do you?" Anna said.

"I have an acting background, you know. I was great as Emily in *Our Town* at the community college. Everyone said I had talent."

Forest snorted. Anna slugged him and he said, "Ouch."

"I'm sure you're very talented, Anna, but—"

"Pretending to be married would be good for you, Tuck," Forest said, leveling him a look. "It'll keep you out of equipment closets with passing women." Forest had been completely disgusted by the Melissa encounter and felt obliged to give the big-brother glare from time to time.

"So, I'll go to the potluck with you," Anna said, getting into it, "and maybe a faculty party at Christmas. I could spend an occasional weekend at your place. There's that candy factory out there I love and some antique stores, so I could get some shopping out of it." Anna scooted to the edge of the sofa in her excitement. "And the rest of the time I'll jet the globe as a pilot. I always thought that would be a great career. And you love a woman in uniform, right?" She batted her eyes at him.

"Good lord."

"Forest, you'll have to take over the boys when I'm in Copper Corners with Tucker," Anna shot at her husband.

"No prob. To help Tuck out I'll be glad to baby-sit."

"Baby-sit? Ha!" she replied with a snort. "How come when a dad takes care of his kids it's baby-sitting? And that does not mean letting them climb the curtains while you watch ESPN, either."

"I can handle it, don't worry."

"I'm starting to love this idea," Anna said. "Plus, I can make sure the principal knows how committed and dedicated and *faithful* you are, right, Tuck?"

"I don't see how this could work, Anna," he said uneasily, but a twinge of hope rose, all the same.

"Call me Julie. And of course it will work. We'll make it work."

"I'll go get the spare ring," Forest said, jumping up.

"I think I know where the negative for this photo is," Anna said, scrutinizing the framed shot, "so we can make a print for your wallet."

"A photo on my desk would be plenty, but…we'd better think this through." Why was he even considering going along with the Forest-Anna steamroller? Only because of his desperation to not look like an idiot to Harvey. He needed the man's confidence in him. And part of that confidence was knowing he was stable and married, not a lying single fake.

"Don't worry, Tucker," Anna said. "This is a good thing. This way you can really be the dedicated guy you want to be. You'll be married to your job. Literally."

Before he could reply, Forest returned, polishing the ring in his shirttail. He plopped it onto Tucker's palm.

There it sat…the symbol of eternal love and fidelity.

That Tucker would be faking. He almost handed it back.

He hated starting out at Copper Corners on the wrong foot—letting the misunderstanding become a false life. On the other hand, it was almost poetic that sex was messing him up again—his last impulsive behavior. This was a warning.

And it was true that being married—even as a pretense—would keep him on the straight and narrow when it came to women. And he'd do such good work that in the end the charade wouldn't matter a bit.

But could a wedding band, a photo on his desk and an occasional appearance by his wife be enough to fake a marriage? Hard to believe. Tucker tucked the ring in his pocket. He'd have to think about it.

2

On his first day at Copper Corners High, Tucker strode purposefully toward the administration building to talk to Harvey Winfield, fingering the wedding band in his pocket as he walked. He'd decided to tell Harvey the truth. He wasn't married. It was all a misunderstanding.

He dreaded how stupid he'd sound, but the fake marriage was too weird, no matter how enthusiastic Anna and Forest were about the idea. This was no way to launch his career. Anna would be disappointed, of course—she planned to drive down tomorrow to organize the house he'd rented—but he had to do the right thing.

Once inside the building, Tucker found Harvey at the reception desk. Perfect. He'd just get it over with and start fresh.

As an idiot.

"Good to see you, Tucker." Harvey shook his hand, gripping Tuck's forearm with his other hand, his eyes warm with affection.

Do it now. Tell him. "I need to clear something up, Harvey."

"Sure thing, but before I forget, your wife called. What a delightful woman. She said to tell you to feel free to work as late as you want, since she has plenty to do at the house. She knows how dedicated you are."

"She does?" he said blankly. Anna must have arrived early and called out here to impress Harvey with Tuck's commitment and her support. Damn, she was good.

"She wanted to know what to bring to the potluck next week." Harvey smiled. "You're a lucky man, Tucker. She reminds me of my Nadine. It's so fortunate that she'll be in town for the dinner. Sounds like the airline keeps her quite busy."

"Oh, yes, she's one busy woman, all right," he said, blowing out a breath. How could he tell Harvey the truth now? His fake wife had sealed his fate. A misunderstanding was one thing, but a plot with coconspirators? With a sigh, Tuck put his hand into his pocket and slid the ring onto his fourth finger. It felt strange—heavy, like the lie pressing in on his chest—but he'd make the best of it.

"Let's get you started," Harvey said. "We've got some papers to sign, of course, but I want you to know right off the bat that I'm going to give you free rein here. I've been accused of being a micromanager, Tucker, but I've turned over a new leaf. The best way to learn this job is to live this job. You'd think after thirty years at it, I'd figure that out. So if you'd keep me posted on your activities—regular updates now—we'll be fine. I know you won't let me down."

And he wouldn't. He'd do everything he could to justify Harvey's faith in him. The fake marriage was a glitch, but he'd just think of himself as married to the job, like Anna had said, and that would have to do.

TWO WEEKS LATER, Tucker saved the changes he'd made in the new computerized class schedule, stood and stretched. He wanted to greet the teachers setting up their rooms early and see what he could do to help them. School would start in a week.

He looked around his office—his first as an administrator. He loved it. The room was tiny, his wooden desk shabby and scarred, his chair in danger of collapsing and his computer practically pre-DOS, but he'd filled the shelves with his own books and professional journals, along with the district's curriculum manuals, hung the walls with motivational posters and artwork, and organized his desk so that the place felt like home.

The brass plaque Ben had given him in high school rested beside his computer. It held a quote from William James: *The greatest discovery of my generation is that a human being can alter his life by altering his attitudes of mind.* That had been Ben's message to him. Tucker liked to keep it always in view.

He'd called Ben about the job, who'd expressed his confidence in Tuck and talked about the things he was working on at Western Sun that Tucker would be able to take over once he got back there. The man Ben had hired was definitely retiring in three years. Tucker had a good shot at the job if he did well at Copper Corners. Things were falling into place.

Every day Tuck had been here made him feel surer this was the right step for him. He was already making a difference. He'd upgraded the class schedule software and purchased a school-wide grading program for next to nothing through a promotion he'd researched. And he was planning to add some needed extracurricular activities right away.

Everything was going according to plan, he thought, looking around again. His glance fell on the photo of him with Anna—no, Julie—his wife. Well, everything except that. He angled the photo out of his line of vision. He would keep that low-key, and it shouldn't matter. Anna would come out to the potluck and then be off on her busy flying schedule.

Grabbing a clipboard to take notes about what the teachers needed, Tucker set off across the quad between the school's brick buildings to meet the teachers who were here—there were three or four at least.

The air was filled with the fierce rasp of cicadas and the sun baked the top of his head. August in southern Arizona was brutal. Its bright burn seemed to have washed out the green of the paloverde tree trunks. Everything looked dusty and tired of summer.

The heat had the opposite effect on Tucker—it energized him. Surveying the campus gave him a rush of ownership and responsibility. This was his school. He knew every corner of campus now. He'd spent a week assisting Dwayne the custodian move shelves and replace equipment in all the buildings, so that helped, but it was more. He'd absorbed the feel of the place, knew all its classrooms and corridors by heart. Sappy, maybe, but there it was.

When he left in three years, things would be better here than when he'd arrived. Achievement scores and student involvement would rise and teacher satisfaction would soar.

Tucker met the new English teacher first, then visited with a veteran history teacher setting up her class. After that, he headed to Building D, where the English teacher had said the new science teacher was working.

As he walked, he found himself running his thumb over the smooth curve of Forest's wedding band. He was constantly aware of it—catching the sunlight when he walked, snagging soap when he washed his hands, in sight when he worked at the computer. Wearing it, he felt phony, but safe. Since he'd declared women off-limits, being married was insurance. He did intend to marry one day, so this was a test of how it would be.

Without the woman. Or the love.

Or the sex.

Which was a definite downside. But he could handle it. He'd sublimate his sex drive in work and everyone would benefit.

He entered the D building, which held science, math, computer and art classes, and got a blast of hip-hop music from an open classroom door—his destination, no doubt.

Inside the room, the music was so loud his ears throbbed. He spotted the teacher on a ladder, hammering something to the ceiling. A jungle vine, he could see, made of cloth. A couple dozen dangled around the room, which was also decorated with three papier-mâché trees.

At the back, there was a bank of terrariums, where he made out a couple of snakes and a large lizard…maybe an iguana? The bulletin boards held maps of South America and photos of exotic creatures. The total effect was of a jungle, dense and complex, and full of color.

And a fire code violation.

Then he got a load of the teacher and lost all thought for a second. She wore white shorts, which were pulled tight over her round backside because of her position on the ladder. Below the shorts were great legs—muscles tensed along their shapely length as she hammered away. Nice feet, too, he saw, since she was barefoot. With plump toes, the nails painted fire-engine red.

She hadn't heard him enter over the pounding music, and now he was close enough to catch her scent. She smelled familiar and sexy…like Melissa. What were the odds of that?

He reminded himself of his purpose here—to offer any help she might need—and called over the music, "Hello?"

"Wha—?" She jerked, then turned, wobbling on the ladder.

Tuck stepped forward and braced her thigh—as firm as it looked—to keep her from tumbling. He looked up at her face and swallowed hard.

Oh, God.

It was Cricket, his college crush, her green eyes round and wide, blond hair in parentheses around her cheeks.

"Tucker! I don't believe it!" Her face lit with pleasure. She looked down at her leg, where his hand still rested.

He let go fast, rubbing his still-warm palm on his pants.

She climbed down the ladder—rather, bounced—twisted a knob on the CD player to lower the volume, then turned to him. "What a small world!"

"Yeah." He felt like Rick from *Casablanca*. Of all the high schools in all the towns in all the world, she had to walk into his.

"You teach here?" she asked.

"I'm the assistant principal. I'm new."

"Me, too. But I'm a teacher. Well, not quite. I have an emergency certificate." She stepped closer to him and he caught more of her special scent—vanilla, cinnamon and something peppery. "They needed a science teacher and I had tons of science credits, plus I love science—I was a volunteer at the zoo, and I've always contributed to the Sierra Club. So, I got the job. Of course, they didn't have another applicant, but, oh, well. Listen to me babble. How'd you end up here?"

"Long story." He didn't care to lay out the details of his fall from grace. She looked as good as he remembered. Short and compact, pixieish, with a heart-shaped face, small nose and pretty mouth—features that made you expect her to be sweet, but he knew she was mouthy and irreverent, with a lusty laugh that managed to charm despite its decibel strength, and green eyes that glinted with mischief.

Nothing she wore was immodest, not even her stretchy red top, but she was so sexy she had to be violating codes all over the place—dress codes, morality codes, building codes, whatever. She was one big violation.

He couldn't help checking out her ring finger and found just a silver peace sign.

"Man, how long has it been?" she asked.

"Must be six, seven years." He tried to sound cool, but he could have figured out exactly how long ago that make-out session had been. It had been two days before Christmas, and they'd drank a couple of beers, talked a long time—finishing each other's sentences—and then they'd gotten personal and there had been that mistletoe....

"Yeah. Finals, right? Christmas time."

"Yeah. Christmas time."

Her eyes told him she remembered the moment, too. And with pleasure, judging by her soft smile. "Whatever happened with you and Sylvia?" she asked. "I moved out just after you and I...after that night."

"Nothing," he said. "I think she married an electrical engineering professor." The guy she'd stood him up for, which made him feel less guilty about kissing Cricket. He'd slept with plenty of women in college, but he never overlapped.

"I lost track of her after I moved out of the apartment," Cricket said. "Too much temptation to party. I had to hit the books, resuscitate my GPA." She scrunched up her nose. "I hated hitting the books."

"I remember," he said. She'd been studying biology when he'd joined her on the couch while he waited for Sylvia and they'd commiserated about GPA pressure and the stifling nature of lecture halls, moving on to discuss a global sweatshop protest they'd both attended, then to their beliefs on social issues—poverty, ecology, the proper role of government.

The words flowed easily, as if they'd known each other for years. They'd disagreed some—Cricket was more black and white in her beliefs than he was—but with humor and mutual respect. In short, they'd connected. Intellectually, emotionally and, um, sexually.

Somewhere in there, she'd started drinking his beer. Then let it slip that she thought he was cute.

And he'd told her she was pretty, and she'd mumbled something about mistletoe, cupped his face with both hands and kissed him...like he was some exotic fruit she wanted to get every juice from.

He'd kissed her right back, a tsunami of lust pounding through him. She'd tasted of beer and peppermint and smelled of cinnamon and vanilla and spice—fresh with a winter bite. She'd slipped onto his lap and he'd held her tight. She'd felt delicate, but springy. Strong and hot.

There was something not to be missed about that encounter. Like snow in Tucson. So rare you had to drop everything and run outside to let the flakes fall in your mouth. Come to think of it, they'd been nowhere near any mistletoe....

"Me, too," she said, taking another step forward. "I remember, too." Electricity zinged between them. He could swear the jungle vines swayed in the static. "We had a great talk. And everything..."

She was looking him over, head cocked like it had been that night right before she'd kissed him. Then her gaze dipped and snagged on something.

His left hand. The gold band gleamed under the fluorescent lights like a treasure.

"You're married?" she said. Did she sound disappointed? And why did he hope so?

"Um, yeah. Absolutely." He twisted the ring with the fingers of his other hand.

"How long?" she asked.

"Two years." Forest and Anna thought that

sounded like enough years to be solidly married and not attract newlywed jokes.

Cricket nodded slowly. "Kids?"

"No."

"But soon?"

"When the time is right." This was true. He did want kids. After he had a real wife, of course. "You're not married?"

"Are you kidding? I'm just figuring out what I want to be when I grow up. When I've got that handled, maybe I'll find someone. When I'm ready to hibernate." She shrugged as if that were unlikely, then tilted her head again. "Is it good? Marriage, I mean?"

"Sure," he said, the lie giving him a twinge. It would be good, he was sure.

She'd obviously picked up his discomfort because she said, "Really?"

"It has its ups and downs," he said to cover his hesitation.

"Yeah. Same with any choice. The pros and cons and ups and downs. I hate that." She bit her lip, then seemed to cheer up. "Anyway, I'm happy for you, Tucker. Really." Her expression warmed, calling back the intimacy of their evening together all those years ago. "She's a lucky woman."

"I don't know about that," he said.

"Oh, I do. You were a great kisser." She elbowed him playfully in the side.

"I'd say that was all you."

"Team effort." She sighed. "That night was something, huh?"

"Yeah. Something."

"I couldn't believe how much I blathered on and on."

"We had a lot to talk about."

"Yeah. A lot."

They stopped talking for a long moment. The beat of attraction thudded in Tucker's ears.

He'd thought about looking her up after Sylvia and he broke up, but they were near graduation, and he'd been disturbed by how powerfully Cricket had affected him. He'd felt out of control, the way he had in high school. Besides, he was too tame for her, he was sure.

With a start, he realized he'd held Cricket's gaze way too long for a married man—even one experiencing ups and downs in his marriage. "Anyway, that was a long time ago."

"And now you're an administrator. Wow. I would have figured you for an ACLU attorney or some intellectual rabble-rouser."

"I considered law, actually, but education is important. It's a way to influence the next generation."

"Sheesh, that sounds ancient. The only generation we're old enough to influence—or even talk about—is the Pepsi one."

"How'd you get into teaching anyway?" he asked, not liking how she made him feel like an old fogy. "Weren't you studying nursing?"

"Turns out blood makes me faint. It's, like, a reflex. I catch sight of red and everything goes black." She shrugged. "Kind of lame, I know."

"You can't help your reflexes," he said.

She smiled. "Sounds better than being a flake, huh? So, after that I tried social work." She made a face.

"No good?"

"Too much bureaucracy. You can save the world, but only after you fill out the correct forms."

"In triplicate?"

"Exactly. Then last summer I was a counselor at a summer camp for low-income kids and really loved it and I realized teaching might be my thing, so I thought I'd see how it goes. Science is cool, too. I love biology. Chemistry's a little scary, but I'll figure it out." She looked around the room, her eyes narrowing in evaluation. "What do you think of my rain forest?"

"Impressive." He'd have to say something about the fire code before she hammered up more vines.

"This will be the framework for teaching biology," she said. "Everything will be tied to this—ecosystems, conservation, the greenhouse effect, species differentiation. Plus, we'll do writing and art projects, along with science."

"A thematically based integrated curriculum."

"Wow." She blinked. "And I just thought it sounded fun."

"That, too."

"So that's how you get the big bucks—coming up with big hairy labels for fun stuff."

"Pretty much. It's a great idea, Cricket. Innovative." *And a fire hazard.* He had to tell her so. It was his job. "The only thing is we can't have anything flammable within six inches of the ceiling tiles."

"What? Oh, right. Good one." She slugged him gently on the arm.

"I'm serious. It's the fire code. And the trees will have to be dealt with, too—the branches trimmed and that one—" he pointed "—needs to be moved so it doesn't block the exit."

"It took me four hours to get this stuff up. And the trees took forever to situate."

"I'll help you move them."

"How about if I just take my chances with the fire marshal?"

"I'm afraid I can't allow that. You'll still have the jungle effect with your animals and bulletin boards."

"Come on, Tucker. You're not one of those rules-are-rules guys, are you? In college, you were at the demonstrations, ready to get arrested with the rest of us."

"We had permits."

"Please, sir, can we protest? Sheesh." She rolled her eyes.

"The petitions and meetings with the university president achieved what we wanted. The demonstrations were mostly to make us feel better."

"That's not true, is it?"

"More or less. The point is that if you play by the major rules, you can bend the minor ones. And safety's major."

"So I'll pat down the kids for matches."

"I'll get another ladder and help you."

"I'll handle it," she said, her eyes sparking with irritation. And stubbornness.

"Okay, then." He lifted his clipboard, pen at the ready. "Is there anything else you need in the way of furniture, equipment or textbooks?"

"What I need is for you to forget the fire code."

"No can do."

They held each other's gaze in a *High Noon* stand-off. Something told him this wouldn't be his last run-in with Cricket.

He blinked first. "Anyway…I know the first few weeks of teaching can be overwhelming, but we're here—Harvey and I—to make your job easier."

She rolled her eyes in a *yeah, right*. But her wry smile softened the effect.

"In the long run, you'll thank me."

"You sound old, Tuck." She patted him on the shoulder.

Part of him bristled, but having her think of him as an old *married* administrator was probably a good thing. If they were in a different place, a different time, he'd be after her in a heartbeat, eager to see if time had altered the heat between them. He rubbed his ring with his thumb, grateful he wore it. Melissa had been a mere echo of Cricket. Without this gold emblem on his fingers, God knows what career-killing indiscretion he'd be tempted into beneath the branches of her papier-mâché trees and the reptilian eyes of her terrarium dwellers. The school board would never buy "Cricket Fever" as a defense at his hearing.

Unless, of course, they knew Cricket.

WHAT THE HELL HAD happened to Tucker Manning? Cricket couldn't believe a guy who kissed like a porn star would stand there like an old geezer and tell her to rip down her jungle. *In the long run, you'll thank me?* Please.

On top of that, he was married. She got a smidge of concern that she was more disappointed about that than she was over her soon-to-be-deforested jungle.

Tucker Manning was married. Unavailable. Taken.

Not that it mattered. Hell, she hadn't seen him in years, though he did cross her mind from time to time. They'd connected in such a warm, easy way that night. She'd felt understood, honored, almost urged to say any outrageous thing she thought or felt.

He'd also starred in some sexy dreams. Maybe because she'd been surprised by how much and how fast she'd wanted him. Major lust had hit at max speed.

Of course, he was hot, with down-slanted, bedroom eyes—George Clooney/Kyle Chandler eyes. And he had this great look—earnest and smart-ass and know-it-all. The boy next door with a Harley and a Mensa membership. Trustworthy, wicked and brilliant. A killer combo.

Plus, his voice was low and confident, with a sexual undertow that sucked her in. Also his mouth was dramatic—sculpted lips, full and so *there*. She'd just had to have a taste…. And wow…. But Tucker had come to his senses, completely mortified and guilty as hell. She could have told him about Sylvia and the professor, but that didn't seem right and she'd been a little shaken up by her reaction to him.

And she still thought about him with lust. Probably because he was The Forbidden. Or maybe because after that night, he disappeared. Or maybe she had disappeared. Whatever. Absence makes the heart more horny? Or curious? Or something.

Now here he was, turning up again like a sexy penny, with that same kissable mouth and all those fabulous features and that thick, dark hair—she'd forgotten about the hair—but he was taken. Locked down. Married. She hoped the woman knew what she had.

On the other hand, he'd turned into an administrator. And not a progressive, authority-sharing one, either. A rules-are-our-friends, by-the-book administrator. He'd probably expect to see her lesson plans for the upcoming week on his desk every Friday. She watched him cross the quad. What a great backside. She was window-shopping only, of course. The man was *married*.

He'd sounded nervous about it, though—*it has its ups and downs*—fiddling with his wedding ring like he wanted to yank it off. She hoped he wasn't unhappily married.

Anyway, enough of the sexual road not taken. She had a new career to explore and no time for good kissers with up-and-down marriages. Small towns meant flat-line on the entertain-o-meter. But that was okay. Her goal was to be the best teacher she could be and really give this career a fair test. Discarding two professions—even if one was because of a physical reflex…good point, Tuck—made her feel, well, flaky.

It was time to get serious. And teaching was it. She was pretty sure. She'd loved the summer camp. Teaching the kids how to boat and ride horses, guiding them through conflicts, shoring up their self-esteem, helping them explore their ideas and interests had been extremely rewarding. She'd felt as though she made a difference in their lives. She wanted more of that. A career of it, in fact.

As the summer ended, she'd recalled that her friend Nikki Winfield's father was a principal. Cricket had worked for Party Time Characters, the kiddie party company Nikki's best friend Mariah had started back then, and had gotten to know Nikki through her.

Before she knew it, Cricket had an interview with Nikki's father, Harvey—a formal, old-fashioned guy, but sweet and completely in love with his school. Her science background and enthusiasm—and the fact they had no other applicants—earned her the job. She would refresh her biology with the textbooks, get teaching tips from colleagues and figure out the chemistry somehow.

The point was that she now had her very own classroom. She had a curriculum to cover, but how she presented it was up to her. She wanted her students to love learning and to figure out how they could make a difference, too.

When she sat still for long, though, doubts assailed her. Was she up to this? Could she stick to it even when it got hard? Would she get hit with the same disappointment she'd felt about social work? Maybe she was too idealistic. She had these great dreams, but the day-to-day getting there wore her down. At least so far.

This had to be different. She felt different. She felt ready. She'd already plowed into it—coming up with her jungle theme for the three sections of biology she would teach. She looked around at what she'd set up. It looked great. Purposeful. Appealing. Exciting. Except now, thanks to Tucker Manning, Fire Code Cop, she had to machete the vines and muscle the trees around.

A surge of stubbornness rolled through her. She wasn't giving up on her rain forest, no matter what Captain Safety said.

Nothing within six inches of the ceiling, huh? Okay, how about seven? If she used lightweight wire extended from the tree branches… She smiled. She'd need some help, though. Out the window, she spotted three kids skateboarding across the campus pathways. She'd get to know them, get their help and annoy Rule Master Manning all at the same time. Talk about multitasking.

She hurried outside to chase them down.

WHEN CRICKET AND THE three students finished the rain-forest renovation, she took them to the town's pizza parlor for food. The garishly lit, green-dragon-themed place was loud with the sounds of arcade games, rich with the tomato-and-baked-bread smell of pizza and decently crowded for a Wednesday night.

They'd just dug into two Chicago-style pepperoni pies and Dr. Pepper in frosty mugs, when Cricket looked up and saw Tucker striding down the aisle between green plastic benches, a bottle of beer in one hand.

"Hey, Tuck," she said, motioning him over. "Join us."

"Cricket." He paused at the end of the table, smiling a great, warm smile that heated her like an electric blanket. "I don't want to intrude." He glanced at the boys, his brows lifted in curiosity.

"Tucker Manning, meet three of Copper Corners' finest sophomores—Jason, Jeff and John, the Triple

Js, as they're known to their friends. Guys, meet your new assistant principal."

Tucker set his bottle on the table and solemnly shook each hand, making enough eye contact to make the guys uncomfortable.

"They helped me rearrange my rain forest. Here, sit." She patted the space beside her for Tucker, since the three students filled the opposite bench.

Tucker took a tentative seat. She could see him measure the distance so they wouldn't touch at shoulder or hip.

Though the boys continued eating, Tucker's presence had definitely put a chill on the meal. The man gave off authority like body heat.

"Are your parents aware of where you boys are?" he said, making it worse. He'd used a relaxed tone, but it came out stern and he'd called them *boys*.

"Pretty much," Jason said, shrugging.

"Maybe you'd better be certain." Tucker took his phone from a back pocket and extended it.

"'Sokay," Jason said. "We should get going, Cricket."

Jeff wolfed the last of his slice and John grabbed a piece to go, leaving three from the second pizza on the tray. She knew full well they would have cleaned up if Tucker hadn't sunk the mood.

"Hang on," she said. "We can talk to Mr. Manning about starting the ecology club."

"That's okay," Jason said. "Thanks, Cricket." The other boys mumbled their thanks, then all three lumbered away.

"Way to be a buzz kill," she joked to Tucker. Despite the distance between them, she felt his body heat and smelled his cologne, a spicy musk that teased like his smile.

Tucker must have noticed how close they were, too, because he slid off her bench and onto the opposite one.

"Was it something I said?" she asked.

"This is better," he said firmly. "And being alone with students at night is not a good idea."

"They slaved over my room. The least I could do was feed them."

"You're young and single and very pretty, Cricket."

"Why, thank you."

"All three of those guys were smitten."

"Nah. It's not me. It was the food. No teen turns down free pizza."

"It just doesn't look good."

"It's okay. It's so noisy we couldn't even hear ourselves flirt and forget playing footsie— the lights are too bright."

His brows lifted in alarm, which reminded her that she'd loved startling him with extreme ideas that long-ago night.

"Kidding, Tucker. Jeez. I'm twenty-seven. That's antique to sophomores."

"I also advise against allowing students to call you by your first name. You need them to respect you."

"Respect has to be earned."

"The kids need a teacher, not a pal. If you're too chummy, they'll take advantage of you, blow off assignments, talk back, refuse to listen. And then you'll end up at war."

Cricket stared at Tucker. He sounded like some tired veteran advising a new recruit how to survive a battle. "I want to reach my students at a human level, Tucker. I'm not their prison guard."

"Too much familiarity is a mistake. Some teachers don't smile for the first month. Maybe that's overboard, but they have a point. Keep your distance, set high standards and you'll give your students what they need—subject knowledge, thinking skills and the self-discipline to get what they want in life."

"What happened to you, Tucker?" She reached across the table to playfully shake him by the shoulders. "Did they brainwash you at administrator school? You weren't hard-hearted in college."

He'd been tender, not tough, that night, and passionate, not reserved, and she'd felt as if she'd belonged in his arms.

She distracted herself from that thought by grabbing Tucker's beer for a big gulp from the bottle.

"Hey!" he said.

"Sorry. It just looked tasty." Which was exactly what she'd said when she'd snitched some of his Corona that night.

Tucker's face stilled. He was remembering the moment, too, she was sure.

"How about some Skee-Ball?" she said to change the subject.

"I don't think so."

"What's a little Skee-Ball between consenting adults?" It was just a light flirt, but their gazes locked like heat-seeking missiles. Fire zoomed through her.

Tucker sucked in a harsh breath, twirling his wedding ring. Again.

As if catching the vibe, a Skee-Ball light began to spin and flash red and the siren blared. *Emergency, emergency. Lust alert. Calling all ice water.*

Cricket crossed her legs to settle herself.

When the sound ceased, Tucker spoke. "I don't think we should consent to anything together, Cricket. There's too much…you-know…going on here."

"You-know?" She couldn't help teasing. "What's you-know?"

"You know what you-know is," he said, low and sexy, his eyes sparkling in the light, his smile crooked, the effect as romantic and inviting in the bright pizza parlor as it would have been in a dimly lit bistro.

She sighed. "Yeah. We both know."

"I'm married. And I'm your boss, more or less. Playing Skee-Ball or sharing a beer or just sitting here talking, however innocent, is a bad idea."

"I hate it when you're right." She leaned forward, chin on her fist. "I hope your wife appreciates you, Tucker."

"I'm sure she does," he said, but his eyes flickered away. What was up with that?

"What's her name anyway? And where did you meet?"

"Her name is Julie and my, um, brother introduced us."

"Where is she tonight? How come you're eating alone?"

"She's out of town. Working. She's, um, an airline pilot."

"An airline pilot? That's cool."

"She likes it."

"So, she travels a lot?"

"All the time."

Why did he look so guilty? She couldn't see Tucker playing around. He struck her as an honest, loyal guy. He'd been very upset about the make-out session while he was still seeing Sylvia. Now Cricket had to know more.

"So what is Julie like?"

"She's smart…and pretty, I guess."

"You guess? Can I see her picture?"

"I don't have one on me."

No photo in the wallet? That wasn't a good sign. She'd figured Tucker would be a sentimental guy, judging from the affectionate way he'd talked about his friends that night. "So, describe her to me."

"Let's see…medium build, dark hair to her shoulders. A little shorter than me." He sounded like he had to wrack his brain to remember.

"That's it? What about her eyes? What color are they?"

"Her eyes?" He looked completely panicked. "They're green…and brown, too. Hazel, I guess."

"Not very observant, Tucker."

"I know the big things."

"Little things add up to big things. Like what's her favorite food? Favorite flavor of ice cream? Best band? What's her pet peeve?"

"The important thing is that we make each other happy."

"Does she make you happy, Tucker? Really?" She hadn't meant to sound so serious, but she was a little worried about him.

"Of course she does," he said, but he seemed tense and he was twisting his wedding ring like a stuck jar lid. "Could we stop talking about my marriage?"

"If you'd rather not talk about it." Maybe Julie wasn't good enough for Tucker. Maybe she'd seen what a catch he was and taken advantage of his kind nature.

"Okay, I'll play your game," he said abruptly, evidently taking her words as a challenge. "Her favorite food is chicken parmesan. Favorite ice cream—Cherry Garcia. She loves Bon Jovi. Her pet peeve is people who chat at the post office window when there's a line. Her dress size is four—six if she feels bloated—and her favorite color is teal. Happy?"

"Teal, huh? Impressive. I didn't think men even knew there was such a color. Of course you could be bluffing," she teased. "I'll check your answers at the back-to-school social. Julie will be there, right?"

"She'll be there, all right." But he didn't look that happy about it.

An explanation suddenly occurred to her. "You don't need to worry, Tuck. I'll keep our cordial past a secret." She winked, then drank another swallow of his beer, knowing it would annoy him.

"Would you like one of your own?" he asked wryly.

"It tastes better borrowed." She was relieved he'd lightened up a little. "I can't wait to meet Julie."

"I'm sure she'll be thrilled to meet you, too," he said, tapping his beer bottle against her Dr. Pepper mug with a sigh.

Maybe once she met Julie, she'd feel better. Find

.out he was in a good marriage with a good woman. She didn't want to think of him unhappy. And she didn't want to be lusting after a married man. Any more than she already was, at least.

3

"THIS FEELS LIKE opening night," Anna whispered, clutching a foil-covered bowl of her Asian chicken salad, which she'd made as Tuck's contribution to the back-to-school potluck.

"Just don't overact," Tucker said for the fifth time, holding the door to the gym for her. Anna was entirely too into her role. She'd quizzed him about the other "characters" who would be part of tonight's "performance," and about her "motivation" as well as his. She'd even done research on female commercial pilots.

"Have a little faith, Tucker. I'm here to help." She clipped her arm through his.

"I know you are." *God help him.* The plan was to meet a few people, grab a quick bite and cut out early. Later, Tucker would watch the twins for a weekend—which would be pure joy—and everything would be back to normal.

With a silent prayer to the patron saint of fake marriages, he led Anna across the gym floor toward where the crowd had gathered by the cafeteria tables covered in patriotic paper cloths.

The gymnasium had been halved by a portable wall to make it more cozy, but voices echoed in the high-ceilinged space. Fluorescent lights gleamed off the polished wood floor and the benches folded against the walls. A cougar glared down from the backboard of the basketball hoop above the stage, where streamers looped, along with a paper welcome banner. The homey aroma of fried chicken, rolls and barbecued beans mingled with the rubber-and-wood smell of the gym for an interesting effect—sporty, yet savory.

Tucker spotted Harvey Winfield near the punch bowl with a woman—his wife Nadine, no doubt—and decided to get the most important encounter over first and fast. "Principal at twelve o'clock," he murmured to Anna through his smile and headed straight for the target.

"So nice to see you both," Harvey said, when they reached him, and had introduced everyone. "Tucker here is my right-hand man," he said to Anna.

"I'm so happy to hear that," Anna said. "Because Tucker simply lives for his work. Just *lives* for it."

"I'm sorry to hear that," Nadine said sympathetically.

"No, no. It's great. Really. Because I live for my work, too, so it's perfect. We're like a well-oiled marriage machine."

Don't over do it, he tried to tell her with his eyes.

"So you're an airline pilot, I hear?" Nadine said.

"Yes, I am. And I love it. Fly, fly, fly. That's my life. And as a woman, it's a wonderful opportunity to blaze a career trail for young women. Did you know that only five percent of commercial pilots in the U.S. are women? Truly shameful. Women have been the unsung heroes of aviation. A woman named Lillian

Todd was designing and building airplanes back in 1906, but no one has even heard of her. The first woman to become a commercial pilot—Helen Richey—didn't get hired until 1934."

"I didn't know that," Nadine said.

"As a matter of fact, according to Women in Aviation International, women now serve in all aviation fields."

"How fascinating."

"But I think that's enough fun flight facts for now, Julie," Tucker said gently. "We don't want to monopolize Harvey and Nadine. And everyone in the buffet line is missing out on your salad." He gave her a look.

"Oh, of course. My salad. I try to contribute where I can, even when I'm away so much. Tucker and I are a true team…even over the miles."

"That's wonderful," Nadine said.

"I am just so happy that Tucker is happy here at Copper Corners," Anna gushed. "And that you're happy with him."

"Very happy," Harvey said.

Harvey and Nadine nodded and smiled.

"We're all happy, Julie," Tucker said, linking elbows and steering her away. "Thanks Harvey, Nadine." He walked Anna away from the crowd to the side of the stage for a quick private consult.

"Where are you going?" she said. "The food's over there."

"Ease up a little, please. You overdid it with the 'we're such a happy, perfect team' stuff. Try to do less talking and more smiling and listening. I'm already sweating buckets here."

"Relax, Tucker. They loved me. And they'll love you because of me. If you're going to pull a stunt, pull it all the way."

"This is my career we're messing with, Anna, not an entry for Sundance. Let me do most of the talking."

"So, I'm supposed to be the long-suffering helpmate? Sharing salad recipes and stain removal tips? That ain't me, babe."

"Anna, please."

"And that's not who you would marry, either. You'd want a woman with spunk and attitude. Someone who would stand up to you, speak her mind, give you hell."

At that moment, he caught sight of Cricket Wilde making a beeline their way, a glass of pink lemonade in one hand, a big grin on her face. Speaking of someone who would give him hell.

Though he dreaded this encounter, his heart leaped with pleasure at seeing her and he wanted to grin back. He forced a neutral expression on his face. "Listen," he said to Anna, low. "The woman I was telling you about? The roommate of one of my girlfriends in college? She's heading over here."

"The one who quizzed you about me?"

"Yes. Don't say a lot. She's already suspicious." He'd had to tell Anna enough so she would go along with his guesses about her favorites, but he'd downplayed their history.

"Trust me, Tuck." Anna turned casually to look at Cricket, who was barreling toward them. "Oooooh, she's darling. You left that part out." She gave him a look. "Very interesting."

"Don't even think it," he said.

"This must be Julie," Cricket said when she was close enough, giving Anna's hand a vigorous shake. "So nice to finally meet you."

Tucker watched her take Anna's measure with those laser greens of hers. He could only pray Cricket would keep her promise to stay mum about the winter kiss. That was the last thing Anna needed to know, with her mind already chewing over attraction possibilities.

Cricket leaned close and scrutinized Anna. "Hazel," she declared and straightened. "You were right, Tuck."

"Tucker told me about your quiz," Anna said. "He did pretty well, except my pet peeve is when really tall people plop in front of you after the movie has started."

"Oh, yeah. I hate that," Cricket said. "And when people crunch their popcorn like fiends during the quiet sequences."

"Yes, yes!" Anna said. "Like pigs at a trough. Why does being in the dark make them lose their manners?" They smiled at each other, newfound allies. No surprise, now that he thought about it. They were a lot alike.

"So, you knew each other in college, huh?" Anna asked.

"Uh, yeah," Cricket said, glancing up at him. "Through my roommate and campus activities. Just passing acquaintances. So, why are you two hiding out over here? Checking for fire code violations? You never know when those crazy Thespians might plug in one too many cords, right?" At least she'd changed the subject from their past, if only to harass him.

"What's this?" Anna said.

"Didn't Tucker tell you how he ruined my rain forest?"

"You ruined her rain forest?" Anna turned on him.

"That wasn't what happened."

"That's exactly what happened. I had the most fabulous jungle vines hanging from the ceiling, with great trees, and he makes me yank everything down."

"No!" Anna said.

"Yes. A fire code violation supposedly."

"It was a safety issue. And I offered to help her fix it."

"Couldn't let him," Cricket said, leaning in to stage-whisper a secret. "I didn't want him to notice the campfire at the back. Not to mention the roast-pig pit."

Anna laughed an entirely too delighted laugh.

"Trust me, Cricket," Tucker said evenly. "If there was a fire, you would—"

"I would thank you, right."

"And this hurts him more than it hurts you," Anna added.

"Exactly," Cricket said, high-fiving Anna. "He wasn't like this in college. Did this happen when he became an administrator?"

Anna surveyed him. "I think he just wants to do the right thing. You know, be careful and conscientious. He means well." She leaned closer to Cricket. "He has an inner rebel. If only someone would set it free…" She winked.

Lord. Was it too soon to leave?

"I'll say," Cricket said. "You should have seen him at the first staff meeting."

"What did I do?" Tucker asked.

"You came on too strong with that 'The Importance of Discipline to Student Learning' speech. You should listen more, lecture less, Tucker. Especially when you're new. And especially in a small town."

"And you're an expert on small towns?"

"I grew up in one. And I know people."

"And I don't?"

"Let me put it this way—if I were an administrator and I saw a new teacher with a lot of enthusiasm, I wouldn't crush her spirit with the rule book the first chance I got. Someone less generous-minded might think you were being an ass."

"If I'd waited to tell you, you wouldn't have had time to fix it before school began."

"You could have cut me a little slack."

"And you should be more careful."

"And what's with the 'older and wiser' routine? We went to school together, Tucker."

"I hate to break in here," Anna said, laughter in her voice and something dangerous in her eyes, "but why don't you take this to the table, Tuck?" She thrust her bowl into his hands. "And bring me a plate of food, please? That would be sweet."

Uh-oh. These two alone would not be good. "How about if all three of us go?" he tried.

"I trust you, darling. I'll just be giving Cricket some tips for helping you be a better administrator. I'll have a thigh and a couple of legs—dark meat. Potatoes, no gravy, corn no butter and iced tea, please. Sweet 'n Low, not NutraSweet."

On top of everything, Anna was a high-maintenance eater. He could hardly yank her away from Cricket. That would look macho and distrustful. He almost wished he'd told Harvey he was Forest's gay life partner. It was beginning to sound safer than having Anna as his fake wife.

"I'll have what she's having," Cricket said. "Except sugar instead of sweetener."

Tucker gave Anna a last hard look—*Don't blow this*—then set off for the food table, determined to make it quick. The pair of them were undoubtedly planning his downfall. From what height, he wasn't entirely sure.

CRICKET LIKED JULIE a lot. She seemed fond of Tucker and certainly took no guff from him. Tucker, on the other hand, was nervous as hell. Maybe because of their college secret. At least Julie didn't know about that. She smiled at her and took a swallow of lemonade.

"So, did you sleep with Tucker or what?" Julie asked.

Cricket choked. Burning lemon shot up her nose.

Julie banged her back. "You okay?"

She nodded, fighting to think—and breathe.

"So, did you?" Julie seemed curious and amused, not worried or jealous.

"No, I didn't…I mean we didn't…"

"But you wanted to, right? You thought about it?"

What was she supposed to say to that? "Well, we were, um, attracted to each other." Julie kept looking at her, waiting eagerly, not upset about the prospect at all. How could Cricket lie to her? The truth was always best. "Well, there was this one time when, uh, we kissed a little, but that was it. And it was a long, long, *long* time ago." She gave a nervous laugh.

"I knew it. The air between you two crackled like Rice Krispies." Julie tapped her nail on her lip, looking almost pleased.

Cricket felt sweaty with tension. "Anyway, I'm sure the reason Tucker didn't tell you was that he was embarrassed. I mean, that was ancient history. He told me you two are happy and everything—"

"But you're still hot for each other," Julie insisted.

"What?" Her face flamed. "No. I mean…"

"It's okay, Cricket," Julie said. "I don't mind. Really." She studied Cricket's face, looking like she had a secret she was dying to share.

Across the room, Tucker was slapping food onto two plates, reaching rudely past people, watching her and Julie as if trying to read their lips. He was no doubt afraid she'd told Julie what she'd just told her. She cringed internally.

"Sometimes Tucker doesn't know what's good for him," Julie said, "so the people who care about him have to act in his best interest. Do you know what I mean?" She spoke speculatively, staring intently at Cricket.

"I guess so…" Cricket said, not sure where Julie was headed with this, but not wanting to ride along.

"I'm going to tell you something really important, but you have to promise not to tell Tucker I told you."

"Maybe you shouldn't tell me. I'm awful with secrets and—"

"Tucker and I are getting a divorce."

"You're what? Oh, I'm so sorry."

"Don't be. We're completely friendly about it. In fact, that's the problem. The way we feel about each other is…like brother and sister. Yeah. Exactly."

"Really?" Cricket felt an instant jolt of sadness for Tucker and a flicker of unhealthy interest in this news.

"Oh, yes. But Tucker likes the idea of being married. We're barely roommates now. He hates change. Frankly, I'm hoping something will give him the courage to let us both move on." She gave Cricket a pointed look.

"Something?"

"Or someone."

"You don't mean...?" Surely she wasn't suggesting that Cricket start something with the man.

"I wouldn't want to presume anything, Cricket, but maybe you can be a listening ear for Tucker."

"A listening ear?"

"Yes. He needs someone to confide in. You're old friends, right? And he obviously likes you. Don't let on that you know anything, of course. If he thinks you feel sorry for him, he'll withdraw. Just be his friend. Listen...commiserate...give advice...or whatever."

"I don't know, Julie." Julie wanted a divorce, but Tucker was hanging on? No wonder he was forever twisting his wedding band.

Right now he was dashing toward them, napkins flying off the plates in the breeze he created. He probably didn't want either of them spilling what they knew. Too late.

"Don't let on you know," Julie whispered.

She nodded just as Tucker arrived and thrust the plates at them. Both held a blob of coleslaw and a single shriveled chicken leg. There were no utensils and the napkins had blown to the floor.

"What are you two talking about?" he asked, his gaze shooting from one to the other.

"I was just telling Cricket that whenever you do the drill sergeant bit with the faculty she should give you a private little salute. To warn you."

"That's it? That's all you said?"

"We said good things, too," Julie said, patting his arm—like a sister, now that Cricket noticed. "We both agree that you mean well and if you'd just go with what you *feel* instead of what you *think*, everyone would be better off."

"My therapist would thank you," he said. "If I had one."

"Is this all there was to eat?" Julie said, examining her pitiful plate. "You didn't even get my salad."

He shrugged. "Sorry."

"Come on, Cricket. Let's show this guy how to work a buffet. Maybe between us we can straighten him out. I'll handle him at home and you take care of him at school. Deal?" She gave Cricket a huge wink.

"I guess…" What did that mean? Be a listening ear about his crumbling marriage? Or more? Surely not. Too bizarre.

Puzzled beyond words, Cricket let Julie drag her to the food table, load her plate and give her the recipe to the Asian chicken salad that she declared Tuck's favorite.

Too weird for words.

4

"GREAT JOB," Cricket said to Jenna Garson, when the sophomore had finished her science-in-the-news report and clumped back to her seat, decorative chains clanking. Cricket kept her tone matter-of-fact, but she wanted to do a victory dance around her desk. The girl, who dressed each day in Goth clothes and makeup, had shown real energy as she read her report—a complete switch from the sullen silence she'd held since school started.

She'd reported on an endangered species indigenous to southern Arizona—the ferruginous pygmy owl—whose cactus habitat was being threatened by phase two of a housing development on the outskirts of town.

This brave, fierce creature, Jenna had concluded, her eyes flashing, her cheeks pink with emotion, *is being wiped off the earth by one terrible thing—insatiable human greed.*

The other students had picked up her fire, Cricket could tell, by the questions they asked, and the outcast girl was suddenly an expert on something other kids wanted to know about.

This was what Cricket wanted—to reach kids like

Jenna, who got lost because they were unusual or quiet or didn't fit in. That and to find a way for the students to make a difference. Hence, the Ecology Now club she'd formed the first week of school. The owl controversy Jenna had reported on would be a perfect focus for the group, and she couldn't wait to get started.

Cricket was proud and excited.

And exhausted.

The bell rang and after the kids had shuffled out, she sank onto her desk, dead tired, her throat raw, her feet throbbing. Thank God this was her last class. She had thirty minutes to rest before her tutoring students arrived.

She lay back on her desk, braced her head on the teacher's editions she'd barely touched—no time— let her legs dangle and closed her burning eyes. No wonder the teachers union fought for planning periods and duty-free breaks. During class she was constantly on her toes and she barely had a chance for a bathroom break in between.

"The nurse's cot would be more comfortable." Tuck's voice, coming from above her, tickled her ears, warm and slow as syrup.

She opened her eyes. He smiled down at her. She smiled back up. *His marriage is failing*, she remembered with a rush of sympathy.

She'd hardly seen him since the potluck. They were both busy with beginning-of-the-year tasks, but she suspected they were avoiding each other. She didn't want to think about what Julie had hinted at and Tucker seemed tense whenever their paths crossed in the lounge or office.

"I was resting until my tutoring kids come in." She propped her elbows on her teacher's editions.

"How are things going?" he asked, concern in his tone.

"Okay, I guess. I'm kinda tired." Light-headed, too, from rising too quickly and being too close to Tucker. She was aware of the streaks of lighter brown in his dark hair, the warmth in his eyes, that crooked grin she liked so much. Luckily, his ridiculously formal oxford shirt and tie served as a solid turnoff.

"Teaching wears you out," he said. "Especially at first. I saw your car here after eight last night. That's late."

"There's tons to do." Her entire life consisted of preparing for class, teaching class or thinking about class, along with tutoring, club meetings and checking papers. She snatched food, showers and sleep whenever she remembered them.

She watched as Tucker glanced above her head, then across her room, taking in the carefully placed trees and vines. He laughed, then lowered his gaze to hers. "Let me guess. You took a ruler to the ceiling and that stuff's just under the limit?"

"You got me." She grinned, eager for the argument.

"Do the kids like it?" he said, not rising to the bait.

"Yeah." They liked to *mess* with it. The concept had backfired a little, though she'd never tell Tucker. The trees she'd so carefully constructed blocked her view of some students, and the rowdy ones enjoyed lodging spitballs in the limbs.

"So it was worth all the trouble then," he said.

"I guess." That was no fun. He hadn't even bristled at her stunt. Instead he seemed supportive and concerned.

"Just don't put too much pressure on yourself," he said.

"I don't have to. Teaching does it for me. You have to track each kid, jab the daydreamers, coax the wallflowers, let the brainiacs spout, but not enough to annoy everyone. It's complicated."

"On top of that, science is a difficult subject."

"Exactly," she said. "How am I supposed to know when to lecture, when to ask questions and how long to wait for answers? Are the kids just spacing or are they thinking?"

"There's an art to it. You learn as you go. It helps if you have student teaching, or at least a class in teaching methods."

"All I've got is an emergency certificate."

"You're at a definite disadvantage. What I could do is take over a few of your classes so you can observe some experienced teachers, see how they work."

"You could do that? I'd love it." Watching other teachers was exactly what she needed. "But do you have time?"

"I'll make time. Nothing's more important than helping a new teacher get a good start."

"Right," she said, grinning. "Much more important than tacking up rule charts and making us inventory supplies."

"Some aspects of our jobs aren't fun. Wait until you have to assign grades."

"My kids are going to grade themselves," she said. She'd read that idea on a teaching methods Web site.

"I advise against it, especially before you really know the range of performance. Parents won't like it, either." Tuck gave her that older-and-wiser look that made her want to go too far.

"Don't be such a traditionalist, Tucker. This will work great. I'll amaze you."

"You already do, Cricket," he said with surprising sincerity and a little longing. His eyes were as warm as a caress. "Just don't burn yourself out. We lose too many good teachers who overdo it, exhaust themselves and give up."

"I'll be okay," she said, liking the tenderness in his expression. "Is that why you quit teaching? You got burned out?"

"I was ready to move on. I wanted to do more—for more kids…and for the teachers. That's where the magic is—those moments between teacher and student when the lightbulb goes on, the fire sparks and the mind opens up. I want to facilitate that, take away the barriers, make it easy for teachers to do their best work."

"Why didn't you say that at the staff meeting? We'd all be kissing your feet."

"I did, Cricket. You were too busy bristling about copy-machine guidelines and equipment inventories."

"Maybe."

"So, anyway, besides letting you observe other teachers, how else can I help you?"

You can kiss it all better. Bad thought. "I think I'll be all right."

"I'd better get back then," he said. Except he just stood there, his eyes holding her, wanting to say more, she could tell.

She could be his listening ear. Her heart began to pound. "Is there something else, Tucker, you wanted to talk about?"

"Maybe." He paused. "Listen, about the other night…"

"Yes?" Her heart pounded harder.

"Anna told me that she mentioned our rough patch."

"Anna?"

He blanched. "I mean Julie. Her full name is Juliana. I call her Anna, too, sometimes." He cleared his throat.

"Okay." He sounded awfully nervous. Must be the marriage crisis. "Yes. Julie did say something." Bam. Bam. Bam. Her heart was a sledgehammer against her ribs.

"I want you to know that we're working it out. Marriage is too important to just give up when it gets a little…um…complicated." His eyes looked as doubtful as his tone was confident.

"What does Julie think about that?"

"Julie? Julie is Julie." He shook his head in exasperation. "She'll come around."

But Julie had seemed dead serious about the divorce. Completely calm and confident. Almost cheerful. Was poor Tucker deluding himself?

"So I'd appreciate it if you'd just wipe that conversation from your mind," he finished. "It was a mistake."

"Certainly." She put her fingers to her temples, closed her eyes and pretended to concentrate, then opened her eyes and smiled, trying not to show the sympathy she knew he'd hate. "All gone."

"Great. So, don't work too late tonight… Oh, that reminds me. I noticed your name on the Campus Climate Committee sign-up sheet."

"I thought it sounded fun." Not really. Tucker had explained the idea as a way to enhance communication and understanding between and among students, faculty, parents and school staff. Everyone thought it was goofy. *Nothing wrong with our climate that a new A/C unit can't fix* was the running joke.

But Tucker had been so jazzed about it that when no one signed the volunteer sheet, she'd put down her name.

"I appreciate your interest, Cricket, but you need to focus your energy on teaching."

"I'll see how I feel tomorrow when it's time for the meeting," she said. But she couldn't stand the thought of no one else being there for him. He wanted to make the campus more inviting to guests, display student work, hang motivational posters and create a peer mediation program to settle conflicts between students. All good ideas that deserved a chance, she thought. Besides, Tucker was in enough trouble trying to save a dead marriage.

"I'll take off then," he said.

They were still standing there looking at each other, breathing in tandem, when three glum freshmen shuffled in.

It took Tucker a moment to come to himself. "Don't keep Ms. Wilde too long," he said to the guys, then smiled at her. "She's had a long day."

AT THREE-THIRTY the next afternoon, Tucker headed toward the faculty lounge where the Campus Climate Committee was to gather before the tour he'd planned. Some committee—just him and Cricket. He'd convinced the librarian and counselor to join the group, but they'd had obligations this afternoon. In desperation, he'd invited Harvey, who'd demurred. *I don't quite grasp your vision on this, Tucker, but I'm sure you'll be fine.*

Sure he'd be fine. He'd be all alone with Cricket after school. Memories of the Melissa fiasco loomed in his mind. At least he'd straightened out the marriage problem Anna had created for him. She sure as hell made a better sister-in-law than a pretend wife.

Tucker rounded the corner to find Cricket bent over the drinking fountain, giving him a stunning view of creamy cleavage, soft lips and sweetly moving throat.

His body on full alert—Cricket lit him up like a pinball machine—Tucker ducked into the workroom and thought about sink clogs and compound fractures to put the kibosh on his erection.

"Tuck?" Cricket stared at him. He undoubtedly looked peculiar, plastered against the wall as if he'd been hiding from someone. Which, of course, he had. "You all right?"

"Just fine. How about yourself?" He shifted so the butcher paper dispenser blocked his body, resting his elbow casually on the roll.

"I'm good. So where's this meeting?"

"I thought we'd tour campus first and decide where to put some welcome signs and display cases. Shall we?" He motioned toward the back exit.

"Shouldn't we wait for the others?"

"There are no others today," he said, clearing his throat.

"So it's just us?"

He nodded and the big institutional clock on the wall clicked five loud seconds while they looked at each other, letting that fact sink in.

"Okay," she said, turning for the door, hips swaying, trailing that sweet, spicy scent that made him think of apple pie and opium dens and orgies....

If only he didn't know what it felt like to kiss her—electric and soft and sweet and hot. Thinking sink clogs, he followed her out of the building.

CRICKET LIKED walking beside Tucker in the early summer dusk. The day's heat had eased and even the cicadas' buzz seemed more relaxed. The campus was deserted, the parking lot empty except for Dwayne the janitor's van, so they were alone—a fact that gave her a shiver of excitement.

Tucker had said he was working on his marriage, but he gave Cricket sideways looks and kept losing his train of thought as they walked and talked. The day might be cooling to a close, but the heat between them was rising.

They reached the first corridor of the D Building, where Tucker wanted to put a student-designed mural, and the only sound in the empty hall was the tap and shuffle of their shoes, the echo and harmony of their voices.

Cricket had a quick mental image of dragging Tucker into a classroom, ripping off his ridiculous tie—and everything else—and going at it. Completely whacked. She was no home wrecker. What was it about him that made her consider something so crazy? The way he looked at her, probably—as if he wanted to race her into that classroom, yanking off his tie as he went.

"I think this is where we should do it," he said.

"What?" Heat rushed through her until she realized he meant the mural.

"On this wall. I think it belongs here."

"Sure. Great. Perfect." She gathered her wits.

"I want the theme to be something about unity and humanity."

"With an emphasis on diversity, I think. The Hispanic and white kids seem to separate into cliques."

"You're absolutely right." He looked at her. "The racial divide is always a problem."

"It was in my high school, at least."

"It's everywhere. I'll talk to the art teacher about the design and have her combine classes and grades to work on it. That should mix up the kids. Working together on a project can break down prejudices if it's handled well."

"I'll be glad to help, too, if you need me."

If you need me? Their gazes tangled, then jerked apart and they stared like idiots at the blank wall.

"Whatever we do, I want it to make students feel like they're part of something," Tucker said. "I don't want kids ever to feel the way I did—lost in the crowd, invisible unless I was in trouble."

"You got in trouble?" she said. "You were, what, rebel with a four-point-oh?"

"Oh, I got bad grades, too, don't worry. If you're going to screw up, do it all the way."

"I can't imagine you screwing up."

"It was a long time ago."

"I bet I would have liked you then."

"If you had a thing for screwups."

"Oh, absolutely."

"I'm not like that anymore."

"I know." She pretended to sigh in disappointment, then decided to be honest. "The new you isn't too bad, when you're not playing warden or auditor."

Their eyes caught again. "I'm glad you understand what I'm trying to do here, Cricket. With the mural...and everything."

"Yes, I do."

Tucker's eyes roved her face, struggling with some emotion. He glanced away and seemed to notice how alone they were. "Let's head back. I want to show you the room I intend to use for the peer conflict sessions. It's a storage area now, but I thought we'd clear it out."

They crossed campus at a businesslike pace, discussing as they walked how to identify the students to be peer mediators. Tucker wanted to make the activity an elective course.

Back in the office, Tuck opened the door to a small room that held a soda machine, a laminator and the refrigerator. "I figure we'll move this stuff into the faculty workroom and bring in a table and chairs."

"It's cozy," she said, stepping inside. It got even cozier when Tucker joined her. Unaided, the door creaked shut behind them. Cricket watched Tuck take a breath that matched hers in shakiness. Light filtered in from a high small window, golden in the gloom.

"So, what happened in high school to make you into a rebel?" she asked to keep the conversation moving.

"My parents' breakup, I guess. They started fighting when I was in middle school and got divorced the summer before my freshman year. They were so angry all the time that they just weren't there for me and Forest, who was a senior and half out the door anyway. At the time I couldn't figure out what family meant or what counted anymore."

"That's tough to go through."

"My high school was huge and crowded, and no one paid much attention when I stopped trying. I mostly skipped class, and when I did attend, I was a pain—showing up with a six-pack, picking fights, causing trouble."

"Did you ever get arrested?"

"Suspended a few times. It was mostly stupid stuff. Impulsive, immature. Then an English teacher—Ben Alton—tracked me down to talk about an essay I'd written that he said showed promise. At first I was belligerent, but he kept at me, and I started writing more and reading and gradually got back into things. Because of him, really. He was a mentor to me."

"Good for him. He saw your potential. Did you keep in touch?"

"As a matter of fact, I got an English degree and took a job teaching at my old school—where he's principal now."

"I bet he's flattered."

"I don't know about that." Tucker got a distant look on his face. There was more to the story than he was telling her.

"Sure he is. You went into teaching, after all. I bet you were a good teacher."

"I tried to be. I cared. And the kids knew that."

"And now you're an administrator. Why not at your old school?"

He gave a start, then cleared his throat. "Eventually. That's my plan. Once I have some experience. I want to do a good job here." His face took on a determined look—almost grim. Some internal engine was driving him hard. "I think I can make a contribution here, introduce innovations, add the extras. A small school doesn't have to be limited." He stopped, then grinned. "Sorry to bend your ear."

"Don't be. I like when you tell me what you're thinking. I always have." Her reminder of their past changed the energy between them, heated it, made it more intimate. They stood very close together in the small room. Now was the time to offer her listening ear. "And, if you ever want to talk about other things…"

"What other things?" He paused, took a harsh breath. "You mean my marriage?" He gave a soundless laugh. "I wish I could, Cricket. I really do." He lifted a hand and, almost as if he couldn't help it, brushed her cheek with the backs of his fingers. "If this were another time and another place…" He leaned closer, then pulled back, as if he wanted to kiss her, but was fighting the impulse.

She could feel the heat of his body, smell his cologne and his skin. She longed for contact, connection, the rush of heat. She began to shake, wanting his mouth, his kiss, the brush of his skin against hers.

"This is killing me, Cricket," he whispered. He put his other hand to her cheek, cupping her face in both hands now.

"You mean the you-know?" she asked.

"Yes," he said, tilting his head. "We can't do this." He moved in.

"No, we can't," she said standing on her toes, tipping up her mouth. It was as if some terrific force field pulled them together.

"This would be bad."

"I know," she said, moving closer. "Very bad." As desperate as she was for his mouth, for that hot, dissolving feeling, she would not be the one who kissed first this time. She couldn't be. He was married. Unhappily, according to his wife, but still. He had to be the one to make the first move.

But he wouldn't do it, she saw.

Oh, hell. She grabbed his face and pulled his mouth to hers.

He groaned in protest, then kissed back, hard, with relief, crushing her to him, and it was wonderful and lush and hot. His lips were velvet and strong and tasted of mint and man—just like she remembered, but better. Stronger, more sure. He seemed to drink her in as if for life itself.

Then he broke off the kiss, shook his head, as if to restore control. "This is wrong. I'm sorry."

Guilt rushed through her at the morose expression on his face. "But I started it," she managed to say.

"Are you okay?" he asked.

"F-fine," she said, dizzy as hell.

"I'll leave now," he said.

"Sure, sure. You go on." She struggled to take in air.

"You sure you're okay?"

"Absolutely." She was about to melt into a puddle on the storage room floor.

"Next time, we'll have the full committee. I promise."

"Good idea."

After he left, she stood there trembling. So much for being a listening ear. She'd jumped right into a kissing mouth.

And, as wrong as it was, all she could think about was doing it again.

5

A WEEK LATER, Cricket drove to Harvey and Nadine Winfield's for the new-teacher get-together in her sputtering, antique VW bug. She wasn't the first to arrive, she saw, parking at the end of a line of cars leading up to the house. Department chairs and their spouses had been invited to the dinner as a way to make the four new teachers feel welcome. She didn't recognize Tucker's car, but maybe Julie had driven.

Cricket headed up the sidewalk, smiling at the tidy white house with its crisply hedged yard. Straight out of *Leave it to Beaver*, as Nikki had put it with a shudder—Nikki wasn't big on traditions or the fifties. Cricket, on the other hand, found the place charming.

The doorbell gave an old-fashioned melodious bing-bong and Harvey let her inside. "Hey, Harv," she said, giving him a hug that embarrassed him. It tickled her to make him blush and harrumph. No one else called him *Harv*, either.

"Welcome to our home," he said, stepping back so she could enter.

Cricket breathed deeply of the scent of fresh-baked bread, mesquite smoke and Nadine's rose-water. "Your home is lovely." She surveyed the living room, filled with tapestry-patterned furniture, a piano, a Hummel-laden curio cabinet, ceiling-high shelves of books and bound magazines.

Photos covered the walls and every surface— Nikki and her older sister at all ages, by themselves and with her parents, then Nikki's sister with her husband and kids. More recent photos showed Nikki with her husband Hollis and their baby boy. The overall effect was homey and academic—like the room's owners.

She looked past Harvey, hoping to see Tucker, but he didn't seem to have arrived. She released the breath she'd been holding.

"Is that our Cricket?" Nadine said, hurrying out of the kitchen for a warm embrace. "You look lovely."

Cricket remembered Nikki telling her about that "smothered in a pillow" feeling she used to get whenever she came home. Cricket could see what she meant—Nadine was intense—but it didn't bother her a bit. Her own mother was timid and ret- icent. Cricket preferred strength—even when it re- sulted in arguments.

"You, too," she said. Nadine wore a June Cleaver apron and, amazingly, pearls.

"How are you liking Copper Corners?" Nadine asked.

"Very much. It reminds me of the town I grew up. Very friendly." She'd been desperate to escape Chino Valley, but that had been more about her parents' limited lives than the town itself, now that she thought about it. She sometimes missed the comfort of knowing everybody and everything about a place.

"We're so glad," Nadine said. "We lose so many

of our young people. I hope you'll give us a chance to show you our charms."

"I'll see how it goes," she said. She couldn't imagine staying here, but she saw the appeal.

"Let's get you some food," Nadine said, hooking her arm and leading her to the dining room table, which groaned under the weight of hors d'oeuvres. "Once Tucker and his wife get here, we'll get started on the meal. The chicken's slow-cooking on the grill."

Tucker. Just the sound of his name gave her a charge. It embarrassed her that she'd let the illicit kiss play in her head all day and embellished it in her dreams at night.

By mutual silent agreement, they'd avoided each other since the kiss, except for the first meeting of the peer conflict resolution group, which had fizzled. They hadn't spoken a private word even then.

Nadine put a floral-patterned china plate in Cricket's hand and began piling appetizers on it. A spring roll, some shrimp, cocktail weenies, chips and guacamole crowded into each other. Then came carrot sticks and broccoli florets.

"I won't have room for supper," she protested, but Nadine plopped two pieces of rumaki on top. "I know how you girls starve yourselves. You can't live on celery and yogurt. I'll pack you up some leftovers before you go."

"Thanks," Cricket said, succumbing to the motherly smothering.

"And, guess what? Nikki and Hollis are bringing the baby up for a visit in a few weeks. She wanted me to tell you about it so you can join her and Mariah for a little catch-up."

"How fun. I've barely seen Mariah. She's so busy at the factory." Cricket had managed just two brief get-togethers with her old friend—one to meet her husband Nathan and their two-year-old daughter.

"She and Nathan are so happy. And that little Angela is a pistol just like Mariah used to be."

"They sure seem happy." Three years ago, Mariah had returned home from Phoenix to convince her former fiancé Nathan not to quit running her family's business, Cactus Confections, which made candy from prickly pear fruit. She'd ended up falling in love all over again with Nathan—and the candy factory—and staying for her own sweet happily ever after.

"Speaking of which, have you met Phil Williams? Our coach?" Nadine winked at Cricket. "Single and looking, I hear."

Oh, yes, she knew Phil. He'd asked her out for a beer "some time," which she hoped never came. His body was impressive, unlike his conversational skills.

Nadine led her to him. "Phil, here's Cricket. I'm sure you haven't had time to talk at school. Why don't you fill her in on your last season. Phil has some very successful footballers, Cricket."

"That's good," Cricket said.

Her food-cramming, matchmaking duties done, Nadine bustled off with a contented smile, leaving Cricket with Phil and a topic she had no more interest in than she did in Phil.

Who was too busy surveying her plate to pick up the conversational ball. "Is that rumaki?" he said.

"Help yourself." She pushed her plate closer to him.

He tugged a rumaki off its toothpick, chewed, and smiled at her. "Beer?" He held out his plastic cup. "I haven't touched it."

"Sure," she said, accepting the drink. "I guess this is our some time."

"Our what?" He munched and swallowed. "Yum."

"Our time to have a beer together."

"Oh, yeah. Sure." He smiled, his brows lifting with surprise. He gave her a speculative look: *First date down, now can we get naked?* It wasn't even sleazy, since he was like a big eager St. Bernard: *Can we, huh? Can we?*

"I don't have much time for a social life. With school, I mean."

"Maybe we could go bowling or hit a bucket of balls. Get physical...well, you know what I mean."

"I'm not much for sports."

"You're not, huh?" He scraped a wad of guacamole onto a chip from her plate, then looked over her body. "How do you keep your weight down eating like this?"

"I share with a friend?" she said, watching him inhale her spring roll.

"Good one," he said, snapping up a broccoli floret.

She glanced across the room, wishing she could join the other new teachers talking with each other and their spouses. Two women and a man, who taught English, history and math, respectively. All were experienced, all were married. Cricket was the only brand-spanking new teacher on campus. And the only single woman, except for the school secretary whose third divorce had soured her on men.

The single men at Copper Corners High included Phil and the band teacher, who was too neat, smelled too good, and knew entirely too much about Cher to be straight.

She sighed and looked up at Phil. Maybe if she slept with the guy, she wouldn't be so hot over impossible Tucker. He was good-looking—a big, healthy hulk of a guy, with a perfectly nice mouth, square jaw, clear eyes. She tuned into herself, waiting for a ping, zing or rush of heat.

Nothing. Zip. Nada.

Phil looked at her expectantly, waiting for her to say something.

"So, you have a good football team?" she said on a sigh, watching for some way to escape.

Phil was deep into an analysis of his players' strengths and weaknesses and the possibilities among upcoming freshmen, when Cricket heard her name called and turned in time for a bruising hug from Julie. Tucker stood at her side, looking uncomfortable.

"You look beautiful," Julie said, standing back to admire her. "Doesn't she look beautiful, Tuck?"

"She looks..." he cleared his throat, "...nice."

"And who's this?" Julie said, meaning Phil, lifting her brows suspiciously, as if Cricket were cheating somehow.

Phil wiped his fingers on his shorts and shook Julie's hand. "Phil Williams. Coach. Nice to meet you."

Cricket introduced Julie.

"Your husband's got us working our tails off, I'll tell you what," he said to Julie.

"Does he now?" Julie said.

"Oh, yeah." Then Phil caught himself. Cricket could almost read his mind. *Insult boss, bad. Praise boss, good.* "But it's great. Real great. We need to get off our lazy duffs and go to some meetings."

"Phil was just explaining about the junior varsity team's potential," Cricket said, grateful for reinforcements.

"Oh, really?" Julie said. "I love baseball."

"Football," Phil corrected.

"That, too. Tucker, why don't you get us some food?" She took Cricket's nearly empty plate and handed it to Phil. "Finish this up, Phil, while we talk, and Cricket can get more."

Cricket made her way to the food table with Tucker, relieved to escape Phil and secretly delighted to be with Tucker, even if it was awkward. They picked up two china plates and stood in front of the rumaki. Neither moved to load food. Instead, they couldn't seem to take their eyes off each other. "You do look great," he said. "Very beautiful."

"You, too." He wore a blue silk sport shirt and khakis and looked so much sexier in casual clothes. The silence stretched and energy zinged dangerously between them. "So...you and Phil hitting it off?" Tucker asked.

"Phil? Hardly. I'm not much into sports."

"Oh." He sounded definitely relieved. Very cute. "So...the peer mediation meeting fell flat, huh?" He was obviously floundering for something to talk about besides each other and what had happened between them in the tiny, gold-lit room.

"Yes. Very."

"What could we do to energize the group?"

"You really want to know?" He wouldn't like this, but it was the truth.

"Of course."

"You have to stop attending."

"Excuse me?"

"It's nothing personal, but you have a chilling effect on the discussion."

"I do?" He sounded almost hurt.

"The kids are afraid if they talk about anything sensitive or controversial, you'll tell their parents."

"I would never do that."

"Of course, but they only know you from morning announcements, severe warnings and detention hall."

"They've told you this?"

"I defended you, but it's a stubborn belief. You're the school muscle, Tucker, even though you're a teddy bear."

"A teddy bear?" He kind of beamed. When he wasn't being a hard-ass, Tucker Manning could be damned charming. "Exactly what sensitive topics can't they discuss around me?"

"Drug issues, drinking, parent conflicts and sex. Mostly sex."

"Sex is a problem."

"No kidding."

He gave her a look and a half smile. "That's not what I mean. Schools are in a delicate position with sex education. Even without me there, you can't have in-depth talks."

"The kids are the ones in a delicate position. Their futures are at stake. They need adult advice."

"But not at school. Unless you want to send permission slips home for the parents to sign."

"Are you nuts? If I could get them to talk to their parents we wouldn't need to talk at school. I think you should—"

"Good evening, Mr. Manning, Ms. Wilde."

They turned to greet Bradford Long, the science department chair, standing ramrod straight, light flashing off his wire-rimmed glasses. He was forever leaning into her room with a finger to his lips, asking for quiet.

Her students were enthusiastic, okay? A quiet room meant death to learning. That's what she wanted to tell him about the pin-drop mausoleum where he droned on about covalents and the Periodic Table.

For once, she welcomed his intrusion, though, since it stopped Tucker from delivering his gag order about sex.

"I wanted to thank you for allowing Cricket to observe your teaching," Tucker said to Bradford. Tucker had taken over her classes and she'd observed several teachers, including Bradford, the least impressive.

"I'm glad to be of service," Bradford said.

"Watching you do the experiment was helpful," Cricket said. Chemistry lab befuddled her a bit, truth be told. She bluffed through the experiments, letting the brighter kids make suggestions, and just urged everyone to record their results and not to be afraid to make mistakes, praying nothing would explode or catch fire.

"Glad to hear it," Bradford said. "And you seem to be doing a better job of lab cleanup." As if that were the only good thing he could say about her. "When we leave the supplies in disarray, others can't find what they need and we waste precious student contact time."

Cricket shot Tucker a look.

"I struggled a little at first myself," Bradford continued, "until I got my material down pat, of course."

And that's the problem, she wanted to say. His classes were all rote lectures, with no spontaneity or student engagement. No life, for that matter.

Bradford was about to expound further on his methods, when a woman arrived at his side. "You're not haranguing these good people, are you, Brad?" The woman turned to Cricket and Tucker. "I'm Helen, his wife." She shook their hands. "That's how he got to be department chair, you know—bossing everyone around. Harvey just made it official."

"Helen," Bradford warned, but his eyes gleamed with affection. He couldn't be all bad, Cricket decided, if this woman loved him. They talked a bit and then Helen and Bradford departed, leaving her alone again with Tucker. A fact she liked too much.

"So, did you tell Julie what happened?" she couldn't resist asking.

"Are you kidding? Of course not. She'd never let me hear the end of it."

"Never let you hear the end of what?" Julie said, appearing beside them.

"Nothing," Tucker said. "Really nothing."

"You were supposed to bring me food." She looked pointedly at the empty plates they both held. They looked at each other sheepishly. "And that Phil is deadly dull. You'd be wasting your time with him, Cricket."

"Dinner!" Nadine's voice rang out, cutting off further debate. Cricket walked with Tucker and Julie out to where two redwood picnic tables had been set end to end with yellow-checked oilcloth and citron candles. Tiki torches planted here and there gave an exotic light to the yard, which backed onto raw desert of mesquite, creosote bushes and a variety of cactus. Cicadas buzzed noisily. Upthrust saguaro and the lacy tops of mesquite trees were dark silhouettes against the pink-and-purple sunset.

Aromatic smoke from the barbecue wreathed the tables, which were loaded with the food Nadine had lovingly prepared. Friendly chatter filled the soft air and everyone smiled in the golden glow of candles and torches. There were some very nice things about small towns, Cricket thought, finding a place across from Julie and Tucker. Some very nice things.

TUCKER WATCHED Cricket slide into place across from Anna and sighed. It wouldn't be easy to sit across from her and keep from staring. Worse, Anna and Cricket were thick as thieves and way too much alike, which could only mean trouble. This would have to be his "wife's" last trip to Copper Corners. She enjoyed it far too much. Thank God Harvey sat at the opposite end of the table, or she'd no doubt have offered to chaperone the Christmas dance.

On the way home, he'd tell her she'd accepted a Far East flying route for an indefinite period of time. She'd be disappointed, but it had to be done. She'd helped him all she needed to. Anything else would be overkill…or a disaster.

Tucker took the bowl of potato salad from the new history teacher sitting next to Cricket, aware of Cricket's lovely laugh, loud and joyous and sensual.

He tried to focus on what the history teacher was saying about the new texts the district had adopted, but he kept glancing at Cricket as she talked with Anna, her face animated, her gestures large.

She was so pretty. The white blouse made her tan dramatic. Her hair was loose and bouncy, her smile easy, always ready to laugh. She practically glowed with energy. He couldn't believe everyone wasn't staring at her.

"Did you hear that, Tucker?" Anna said, jabbing him in the ribs.

"Mmm?" he blinked and turned to her.

"Cricket's taking her ecology club to the zoning hearing to defend the ferra-whozit pygmy owl."

"Ferruginous pygmy owl," Cricket said. "Only seven inches tall and very shy, but it can take down a bird twice its size and it eats scorpions."

"That's one tough itty-bitty birdie," Anna said.

"But vulnerable to man. The stand of saguaro where they're building Phase Two of the Copper Basin housing development is home to twelve. There are only some fifty known to exist anywhere in the world."

"So, Cricket's taking the kids to testify in their defense," Anna said. "Isn't that cool?"

"I don't know, Cricket. That's a highly charged, political situation." He'd read the newspaper, too, and knew that community sentiment supported the builders.

"It's also an important science issue," Cricket said. Her eyes threw sparks and her chin went up.

"Then I hope you intend to approve what the students say."

"I'll make suggestions. But it's up to them. Remember the First Amendment?"

"It's not that simple. We have a responsibility—*in loco parentis.*"

"Ooh," Anna said. "Isn't he sexy when he speaks Latin?" she said to Cricket, who grinned.

"I understand the appeal of the project," he continued, "but, as a new teacher, you do not want to become embroiled in a controversy. You should exercise caution."

"Caution never accomplished anything important," Cricket said, her eyes sparking in the candlelight.

"Right on," Anna added. "Well-behaved women rarely make history."

Cricket gave Anna a thumbs up. "And how does that famous quote go, 'Never doubt that a small group of thoughtful committed people...or was it individuals?...can change the world. Indeed...'" She paused, looking for rest of the quote.

"'...it's the only thing that ever has,'" he finished with a weary sigh. "Margaret Mead."

"So you're with us?" Cricket said, tapping her lemonade glass against his. "Solidarity, forever?"

"I'm saying, manage the situation. Guide the students and don't let them get too deeply into this."

"I remember we did a save-the-dolphin thing when I was in middle school," Anna mused, "and some right-wing legislator accused my teacher of being a communist. That stunk. Our poor teacher. She actually cried in class. I still remember that."

"My point exactly," Tucker said. "We don't want you to end up in tears, Cricket, right?"

"This is for my own good?" she said, her tone teasing, her eyes twinkling with mischief.

"This hurts him more than it hurts you," Anna added, winking.

"When you're older, you'll thank me," Cricket threw in.

The pair leaned over the table, laughing. At him.

"You two are dangerous," he grumbled, meaning it, but wanting to laugh all the same.

"Well, I'm off to the rest room," Anna said. "On the way, I'll tell Harvey that you're keeping your eye on Comrade Cricket, the Red Menace in the science department."

God was definitely not having mercy on his soul.

"We're just teasing, Tucker," Cricket said.

"I know." And that was the problem. This was a serious situation, but he couldn't make that clear when he kept falling under her spell. All his persuasive powers, all his authority, melted away in the face of her energy, her determination, her irresistibility. He just hoped she had enough sense to take his advice. And that he had sense enough to make sure she did.

CRICKET WAS DOWNING the last bite of homemade shortcake topped with homegrown strawberries, when Nadine stood and announced, "Into the living room for Pictionary!" as if leading a battle charge.

"Not the games," someone groaned in playful complaint.

"Yes, the games," Nadine replied.

Cricket loved games, so she stood to follow her hostess.

Except before she got far, Julie grabbed her forearm, fingers like a vice. "We have to talk," she whispered, then called loudly, "Cricket and I will wash up, Nadine."

Tucker tried to help, but Julie shooed him away and she and Cricket were soon busy washing the serving bowls and pots at the sink. Julie handed Cricket a casserole dish to dry, looked around to be sure they were alone, and said, "Okay, what happened with you and Tucker this week?"

"Huh?" Cricket nearly dropped the dish.

"And don't say 'nothing' like Tucker. He turns bright red whenever I mention your name."

"I…well…look, Julie, he wants to work things out with you. Don't you think you should give it a chance? Maybe consider couples therapy?"

Julie laughed, then shook her head. "You are so sweet." A cell phone trilled and she pulled it out of her pocket. She looked at the display, then grabbed up the leftover bags of potato chips and rolls. "I'll put these away," she said and headed for the pantry, speaking into the phone as she went.

A few minutes later, Cricket carried the dishes she'd dried to the cupboard. Crouching to put them away, she could hear Julie on the phone. She didn't mean to eavesdrop, but Julie's words made her freeze.

"I love you, too," she was whispering, her voice

lush with intimacy. "Just be patient. I'm working on it....I miss you, too...What? Use the lotion. Rub it in. Yeah, all over.... Did I ever tell you how sexy you are when you do that? Mmm. Great. I *am* doing the right thing. I love you. Bye."

Cricket was stunned. Poor Tucker was trying to save their marriage, while Julie was in the pantry having phone sex right in the middle of Tucker's faculty party. With lotion, no less. Cricket was still crouched, a saucepan in one hand, when Julie emerged from the pantry and nearly tripped over her.

"Cricket! What are you...? You heard me?"

Cricket stood. "You have to talk to Tucker about this. It isn't right."

"Oh, hell," Julie said, sounding more annoyed than sheepish. "Tucker will kill me, but now you have to know the truth. Come here." Julie tugged her into the pantry.

Distantly, Cricket heard laughter and exclamations from where she wished she was right now—playing games and having fun, instead of shut into a pantry listening to the confessions of a cheating wife.

A cheating wife she really liked, too.

"Swear you'll tell Tucker that you *forced* me to tell you this," Julie said.

"What? I put a pot to your head?" She raised the one she still held. Julie seemed positively cheerful about all this—the adultery and the confession. Poor, poor Tucker.

"I'll take that as a promise." Julie took a deep, happy breath. "Here goes. The man I was talking to just now?"

"Yes?"

"He's my husband."

"Your what?"

"My husband. Tucker's brother, Forest."

"Tucker's brother?" Cricket stared at Julie.

"It's a long story that Tucker can tell you, but the basic deal is that when Harvey offered Tuck the job, a woman he was sleeping with answered his phone—Julie—and Harvey assumed she was Tuck's wife. Tucker thought it would be best if he didn't correct the man. Small towns and single guys and all that jazz."

"Small towns and single guys?" What was she talking about? "But you're Julie, too…"

"No. I'm Anna. I offered to pretend to be Julie—his wife—to help him out, make a good impression. He really didn't want to do it, but I convinced him. And then I met you and I kind of hoped…well…that kismet would take over."

"Kismet?"

"Yes, and now that you know, maybe it can. Take over, I mean."

"And the man on the phone with the lotion was your husband?"

"Yep. He was getting our boys ready for bed and he needed help. Why do men pretend to be incompetent with children?"

"You and Tucker's brother have kids? And Tucker's single?"

"Free as a bird. So now you can tell him you know and let things happen. You'll have to be discreet, of course, because everyone thinks he's married. I don't know what you want to do about that, but I'm sure we can work something out."

Cricket was stunned. "Why didn't he tell me?"

"I thought he might. But he's got this idea he has to be careful and serious and focused on work all the time."

"I see…." She thought about Tucker holding up his ring to her like a cross to ward off a vampire.

"I'm not telling you what to do or anything, but I'll be happy to pretend to run off with a copilot or a straight male flight attendant so you two can get together."

"Huh?" She shook her head. "No. Don't. Please."

"Too soon, right? Just talk to Tucker. This whole thing wouldn't have been an issue except for Melissa."

"Melissa? Who's Melissa?"

"A woman he went nuts for where he used to teach. He'll tell you the rest when he tells you about Julie. We better get back out there."

The rest? What more could there be? Melissa and Julie—no, Anna—and lying about being married was plenty. Cricket plopped down on a brown plastic bag of potatoes, still holding the saucepan.

"Are you all right?" Julie-now-Anna asked.

"I've got to think about this," she said.

"Sure. But hurry. Sounds like they're playing charades."

Charades. Right. Tucker had been playing that since the day he'd grabbed her thigh on the ladder. No kidding. And he'd stuck with the story ever since. Even in that storage room, kissing, rocked by lust, he'd kept up the pretense.

That hurt her feelings.

And irritated her.

And made her wonder how far she could tempt him.

6

CRICKET SAT IN THE back seat of Tucker's car, once again a victim of a Julie/Anna plot. The woman had announced to Harvey they would drop Cricket home, since she'd been drinking. A single beer was all she'd had, but she wasn't about to make an issue of it, and now she sat in the back seat with the three foil-covered plates of leftovers Nadine had forced on her. Why was everyone so intent on feeding her?

Still mulling over Julie's startling revelation, she was glad to be going home. She needed time to figure out what she wanted to say and do about Tucker's big secret.

"I'm reeeeally tired, Tuck," Julie said from the front seat. "Drop me off first, would you?"

"Drop you off?"

"It's on the way. Then you can take Cricket home."

The woman was still maneuvering. She wanted Cricket to talk to Tucker, no doubt, but she wasn't ready yet. "That's okay," Cricket said.

"I don't think that would be good, darling," Tucker said. *Darling*? That sounded so fake. How had she ever been fooled?

"Sure it would, Tuck," Julie said. "It would be great."

"I think Cricket's very tired, aren't you, Cricket?"

Now he was putting words in her mouth. What, was he afraid of her? She was suddenly sick of being pushed and tricked. She wanted to do a little maneuvering of her own. "Not at all, Tucker," she said. "Drop Julie off first and let the woman get some rest. Then you and I can talk."

"Talk?"

He glanced anxiously in the rearview mirror and his hands tightened on the wheel. She just smiled sweetly back at him. *We'll talk, all right. Just you wait.*

WHAT THE HELL WAS Anna up to? Tuck wondered. Cricket, too. The pair had spent a long time together in the kitchen. What had they talked about? Cricket's eyes in the rearview glittered at him with an odd light. He swallowed hard.

Maybe he should just tell her the truth. But she'd think he was an idiot and never let him hear the end of it. Besides, if she knew he was single and he knew she knew, he could see them going at it like Tasmanian devils or minks or bunnies or some other highly sexed creature. And he'd be in worse trouble than ever.

They let Anna off at the house, and Cricket climbed in the front seat beside him, her skirt sliding a delectable distance up her thigh.

To distract himself from the bulge behind his zipper that she'd inspired, Tucker kept the small talk going all the way to the Friendly Wheels Trailer Village, where Cricket lived. They discussed the barbecue, the faculty, her department chair and pygmy owls. Finally, Cricket directed him to a round-cornered silver Airstream, and he braked.

She hopped out of the car and came around to open his door, foil-covered plates in one hand. "Come in and I'll make you some coffee."

"I'd better get back," he said, reaching for the door handle.

She hung onto the edge of the door. "What? Are you scared of me, Tucker?" Her bent-over position revealed way too much of the tops of her breasts.

"It just doesn't look right."

"Come on. I dare you. It's just a cup of coffee. Maybe some more of Nadine's shortcake. I grind my own beans…."

"I'll bet you do. That's very appealing, but…"

"But what? You afraid I'll show you my, um, endangered species chart?" She waggled her brow at him, making him want to laugh—and kiss her. Everywhere.

"Come on, Tucker. I promise not to attack you."

Oh, for Chrissake, he could have a cup of coffee with the woman, if for no other reason than to get that *you can't handle me* smirk off her face. He could control himself. He rubbed his magic ring with his thumb.

The inside of the trailer was a visit to the sixties. The walls were a dizzying pink with huge daisies painted everywhere. Accents were in a lime green so bright it stung. That combined with the lush cinnamon-vanilla scent in the air created an overwhelming sensory assault.

"My chart," she said, gesturing at a huge poster of animals pinned to the wall behind her screaming-green velour sofa.

"Very nice." He glanced at it, then at Cricket, who was staring at him.

"You know what I said about not attacking you?" she said, looking at him like she wanted him as her after-dinner treat.

"Yes?"

"I lied." She put her arms around his neck, pushed him backward onto the sofa and began kissing him.

"What are you doing?" he said, breaking away.

"What does it look like? Attacking you."

"We can't do this."

She only shifted to sit on his lap. "Why fight it, Tucker? You're only human. You know this is what you want." She grabbed his hands and slid them under her blouse where he was startled to find no bra, just firm breasts with raspberry peaks.

"But…I'm…married," he groaned, kissing her between words, arousal roaring through him.

"If you show me that ring again, I'll scream."

And then he was lost. They were on that college couch all over again, with her incredible lips on his, her fresh scent filling his head. And this time he had her breasts in his hands, her nipples between his fingers and nothing to stop him from pursuing more.

He tasted inside her mouth with his tongue, and gently squeezed her nipples, a move that seemed to electrify her. She moaned and trembled. He kept at it, touching her the way he'd wanted to touch her back then, but hadn't dared because of Sylvia.

Wanting more contact, he slid one hand from the glory of her breasts to find her through her panties, damp and warm. He pressed her, then slid the length of her sex with his finger.

"Oh," she gasped, breaking away to look at him,

her eyes wide, as if this hadn't been quite what she'd expected.

He reached beneath the fabric where she was swollen and wet and silken to the touch.

"Oh, yes," she said and sank into the feeling, moving against his fingers, helping him know what she liked.

He stroked and teased her there, rolling her nipple between two fingers of his other hand.

She writhed against his fingers below and arched into the hand above. "Oh, this is so good," she breathed. "I knew you would be good. Sooo good." Her movements became frantic, and he sensed she was close to climax.

Abruptly, she cried out and collapsed onto his chest, jerking and gasping for air.

"Cricket," he said, releasing her breast to stroke her hair, so happy he'd pleased her. He moved his lower hand slowly away from her parts.

"Wow. That was intense." She sounded confused and a little uncertain. She pushed her hair away from her pink cheeks, smiled with her kiss-bruised lips, and collected herself. "Now, it's your turn," she said, going for his zipper.

Yes. Yes. Why had they waited so long? He wasn't married, after all…

Except Cricket didn't know that.

He froze, then caught her hand before she could touch him mindless. "Stop. This is wrong." He lifted her off his lap and set her one couch cushion away. He zipped himself, then leaned forward, resting his elbows on his knees, his head into his hands. "I'm so sorry, Cricket. What you must think of me."

THIS WAS NO FUN at all, Cricket realized, seeing how devastated Tucker was that he'd succumbed to her assault. The poor guy hadn't even gotten an orgasm before guilt overwhelmed him.

She'd only meant to get back at him a little for lying to her—give him a taste of his own medicine, remind him that he wasn't perfect. Except he'd gotten her so charged up so fast that she'd collapsed into a whopper of an orgasm. Now *she* felt guilty.

"I really am an honorable person," he said, anguish darkening his gaze. "I have to explain something, Cricket. You deserve the truth."

He was going to confess.

"You don't have to, Tuck," she said.

"Oh, yes I do," he said. "You see, I'm not actually—"

She put a finger to his lips. "You're not married. I know."

"Julie told you?"

"Anna told me. Yeah. I overheard her talking to her husband on the phone. I thought they were having phone sex, actually, but it was bath time for the kids. Anyway, she told me the situation."

He sighed. "I knew this was a bad idea from the beginning."

"Why didn't you just tell Harvey you weren't married? He's surely aware that people sleep together."

"It's a long story."

"Something about Melissa, right?"

"She told you about Melissa?"

"She said you'd tell me." She put her legs across

his lap, her arms around his neck, cuddling up. "So tell me."

"Do I have a choice?"

"None whatsoever," she said, running her fingernail along the edge of his ear.

He shuddered in response, which gratified her. "I give." So he told her about Melissa and getting caught by the volleyball team and losing the job with Ben Alton and how he had to prove himself at Copper Corners and especially stay clear of sex scandals. And about Julie answering the phone and refusing to even consider a drive-thru Las Vegas wedding. He managed a laugh at that part.

"I would have been fine, too," he finished, "if you hadn't shown up and been so impossible to resist."

"Sorry," she said, not sorry at all.

His eyes roved her face, then lower to her breasts. He sighed, like a dieter looking in a bakery window.

"Go ahead," she whispered. "They're all yours." She put one of his hands under her shirt and onto her breast.

Desire flared in his eyes and his erection moved against her leg. "You're killing me, Cricket," he said, then smiled wryly. "And if you keep it up, you'll kill my career, too."

"It'll be fine. I'm the only one who knows. And I think it's time you got that *coffee* I promised you."

"Coffee?"

"Not coffee...*coffee*." She emphasized the last with a waggled brow. "You gave me a quick cup of *instant*, already, but now we can take our time and I'll make you a double espresso grande with cinnamon and whipped cream on top."

"What about your neighbors?" He indicated the window to their left.

She reached past him and slapped the light switch off, letting moonlight bathe them in a gray glow. "There."

"But my car's parked right on the street."

"So you leave before Mrs. Thompson takes her Pekingese out to pee," she said, kissing his neck. "We have until dawn."

"What am I going to do with you?" he asked, threading his fingers in her hair. "You kiss like you invented it and all I can think of is how you feel and smell and taste." He leaned in and barely brushed her lips, a kiss like a whisper, making her feel like a not-quite-al-dente noodle. "But if I get caught up in this, you'll be all I'll be able to think about."

"This will clear your head so you can focus better at school," she said, kissing him back, teasing his lips with her tongue, but she could feel him withdrawing.

"No. I can't do it. I'm a married man in the home of a single, non-certified teacher that I supervise, no less, after 10:00 p.m. with the lights off. This is a little town. They'll know whether I buy ribbed or smooth."

"Luckily, you don't need either. I'm on the pill and as long as you're disease free, we're good to go."

"That's not the point—though I'm healthy, just so you know." He cleared his throat. "I've already used poor judgment, Cricket. This has to stop. Here and now."

He stood, straight and tall, the twinkle gone from his bedroom eyes, his smart-ass smile now straight as a string.

Cricket's sexual heat cooled like Magic Shell on ice cream. Emotions rose and faded quickly in her, and it looked like she was finished with Tucker Manning. Her reaction to him had been a little extreme, anyway. She wasn't slow to climax, but she'd practically exploded at his touch.

Something about how delicious it was to be in his arms. There was a rightness to it, like they were built for each other. She didn't feel as if she had to perform or adjust or test the waters or try things out. However she wanted to touch him or he her would be just right.

It was probably the thrill of the forbidden—in college, after all, he'd been taken by Sylvia. And now, he was married. Sort of. That which is denied must be had.

And she'd had it, she told herself. Conquest attained. Mountain scaled. River forded. Done and done.

Except he hadn't been inside her. She hadn't felt that glorious helpless moment of his release. They hadn't been naked together, slippery with sweat, reveling in their bodies for hours and hours. There hadn't been those whispered confessions of need and want.

Uh-oh. She was getting all wiggly again. And she didn't want him to see that. She rose and lunged for the door, opened it and stuck her head out, pretending to check both directions. "Coast is clear," she whispered theatrically. "If anyone asks me, I'll say you were working on my plumbing. No, make that my wiring…yeah, wiring. I'll say I had a short and you closed the circuit."

"I don't mean to hurt your feelings, Cricket. I just think it's best if we cool it."

"Please." She raised her hand in a stop sign. "It's fine. You're right. I'm just sorry it wasn't good for you."

"It was great for me. And at another time, another place…"

"We'd rock each other's world, I know," she said. "I understand your position. This could be messy because of your job and your history. I get it." Though it did irritate her how easily he got control of himself. She was still pretty shaky, even though she'd climaxed. He should be wound tight and rock hard.

She also didn't like the way he sneaked away with his headlights off, like a criminal escaping the scene of a crime.

That's probably how he thought about it. A crime. For her, the crime was quitting before they'd even really gotten started.

MIRIAM FELDMAN, president of the Ecology Now Club, read the newspaper story out loud to the club members sitting around the table in Cricket's room. "'Calling it pygmy owl genocide, students from Copper Corners High gave impassioned speeches against Phase Two of the Copper Basin housing development at last night's zoning commission hearing,'" she read. "I said that about the genocide. That was my speech." She beamed at the group, reminding Cricket of herself at that age— filled with passion for justice and the underdog.

"Keep reading," her boyfriend Jason said.

"Okay. 'Alleging the housing project will destroy the habitat of the rare ferruginous pygmy owl, an endangered species believed to nest in the saguaros where Bluestone Development plans to launch Phase Two of construction on Copper Corners' east side, the students called for an environmental impact study. The teens who packed the audience created such uproar that the commissioners voted to continue testimony at their next meeting.'

"Here's your part, Cricket," Miriam said. "'Copper Corners students have every right to participate in civic activities,' said Cricket Wilde, science teacher at the school and sponsor of the Ecology Now Club. 'Now they can see that they have a voice—that they can be heard.'"

"Great quote," Miriam said. The other students in the room nodded.

Cricket felt queasy. The news story left the impression that the school had endorsed the students' comments. Harvey and Tucker would not like that, or the rest of her quote, which read more belligerently than it had sounded last night.

A voice rang out over their heads. "Ms. Wilde?"

Tucker on the intercom. And he didn't sound happy.

"Are you in trouble?" Miriam asked her in a whisper.

Very likely. "Yes?" she called into the air, as if to God.

"Can I see you in my office, please?"

"I'm in a meeting right now."

"Afterward, then."

"Fine." He definitely had a bee up his Dockers.

"So, where were we?" she said to the students, trying not to feel nervous. It had been a week since their encounter in her trailer, and Tucker and she had steered clear of each other, though she thought of him often. Too often.

"If the pygmy owl could talk it would thank us," Jenna said softly.

Heads turned to look at her. This was the first time Jenna had spoken in a meeting without being asked a question.

"Exactly," Miriam said.

Jenna blushed. This was good for her, Cricket realized, and reminded herself to touch base with the girl about the first draft of her science report, which needed work.

"What we did was important," Miriam said. "We spoke out for creatures who can't speak for themselves."

The students pondered that statement for a quiet moment, pride as thick as smoke in the room.

The students talked about next steps, deciding to circulate "Save the pygmy owl" petitions at school and in town, and Miriam would ask her father to ask the lawyer he knew about filing a lawsuit to stop the development until a more thorough environmental study could be done.

Cricket felt a little like Pandora, not quite sure about the box she'd opened, but the students were so fired up she had to support them.

At the end of the meeting, as the kids left, Cricket called Jenna to her desk. "Your paper is shaping up," she said, locating it among the reports on her desk. She turned it toward Jenna. "You just need more facts to support your arguments."

Jenna dropped her gaze to the floor. "You said to write what I felt," she mumbled.

"But you have to use data to back your claims. When you use facts *and* feeling, you have more power to persuade."

"Oh." She nodded at the floor.

"I'm on your side, Jenna. How can I help?"

"I just don't know how to, um, find more facts." She glanced up at Cricket, then down. "Our computer at home is busted."

"How about our library? I'm sure the media specialist would be glad to help you."

"She's always busy."

But she was easy to talk to, Cricket knew. She studied Jenna's face. Without a boost, the girl would clearly let this slide and Cricket would be forced to give her a discouraging grade. "Tell you what. I'm in the library most Wednesdays after class. Maybe I can give you some tips."

"You would do that?"

"Sure."

"Cool," she said, her cheeks pink beneath the deliberately pale makeup. "I'll be there." She headed off with a bit more energy in her combat-booted steps.

This was progress. Cricket had enticed Jenna to the Ecology Now meetings, given her a chance to speak up, and now she would teach her how to do research. The girl was blossoming right before her eyes. This was what teaching was all about.

Not even getting reprimanded by the assistant principal could dent Cricket's satisfaction. She straightened her shoulders and marched off to face the music...chewing her lip as she went.

She was nervous, for sure. Only six weeks into

school and she had a reputation as a rabble-rouser. She didn't have tenure or even a teaching credential. If she wanted to stay in the classroom, she had to keep Harvey and Tucker on her side. Plus, she needed Tucker's approval for what the peer mediation group planned.

The kids wanted to turn their discussions about sex and the pressure to have it into skits—role plays they would perform for the entire student body. She had to get Tucker to okay the plan. Today, however, would not be the day to bring it up.

It was probably good that Tucker and her were about to have words. She couldn't figure out why she was so hot for him. He wasn't her type—too strict, too conservative, too father-knows-best. So why did she *long* for him?

Maybe she just needed to get laid. She was going to Tucson with Mariah on Saturday to hear her husband Nathan, who had a guest gig playing sax—his hobby. Maybe she'd meet someone at the bar. Outside Tucker's office she spotted Coach Phil.

"Hey, Cricket," Phil said.

What about him? Nah, she decided as she waved at Phil and kept walking. She wanted someone she could lock horns with…then screw his brains out. Someone like the infuriating guy behind this door. With a sigh, she tapped on it.

TUCKER SENSED Cricket's presence before he heard her talking to Phil Williams, who was definitely hitting on her. He hoped she knew that the guy was an idiot.

He shouldn't care, of course. It was none of his

business. He'd stayed clear of Cricket since that indiscretion in her Airstream on her Day-Glo sofa. Walking away that night had restored his faith in himself, even though he'd lain awake until dawn, his car keys within reach, dying to drive back to her arms and her undoubtedly bright pink or green bed.

Now he would see her here in his office, face to face, body to body, all alone. His heart pounded in his chest like a kid with a crush. He couldn't get the touch of her out of his mind, or the way she'd moved against his hand, or the sound of her voice when she'd cried out.

The conversation he was about to have with her should kill all that, though. He picked up the folded newspaper. Harvey had circled the article about the zoning hearing in red and written *See me re: this* on it. The mayor and two town councilmen were angry about the story, according to Harvey. Plus, the school board president was the attorney for Bluestone Development. Tucker had to get Cricket to cool it.

Someone tapped on his door—fast and sharp— Cricket for sure. He reached to open the door, but she'd already done it.

"Hello!" she said, seeming startled at how close he stood. "You wanted me?"

Yeah. Naked. "Have a seat." He turned and strode to his desk to hide the evidence of the effect she'd had on him. Just a glance or a whiff of her turned him to stone below decks.

Cricket sat in the chair across from him. "So, what did you want me *for*?" she asked, her breasts swelling upward with her sigh, as if to say, *come get me, touch me, taste me*. But she wasn't flirting with him. She was nervous.

He cleared his throat and held out the newspaper, tapping the circled article.

"I read it," she said, not accepting it from him. "Is there a problem?" Despite her defiant tone, she looked worried.

He read from the article. "'If we can't help our students stand up for what they believe in, what is our purpose as educators?' Did you say that to the reporter?"

"More or less," she said, wiggling in her seat in a way that sent a charge through him. "But it reads worse than it sounded."

"I spoke to you about this, Cricket. As a new teacher, you have to be careful. The school board and the town council are quite upset about the students' actions."

"It was a learning experience, Tucker. I know you can see that. It meant a lot to the students."

"Forget public protests, Cricket, and focus on the classroom. Sponsor a debate about the issue in class. Invite the developers to present their side."

"The kids want to do something. They want to make a difference."

"So, raise money for an environmental cause—rain forests or whales. Serve meals at a homeless shelter. Do something meaningful that isn't controversial."

"Don't tell me, let me guess—this is for my own good." She sighed and he could tell she was giving in. She looked up at him. "Okay. I'll talk to them. They're getting petition signatures and talking to an attorney about legal possibilities. Maybe that will be enough."

"Forget legal action. Stick with the petitions."

"But—"

"You can help the students without putting your job on the line."

"I get it. Okay."

"I'll tell Harvey your plan so he can calm down the school board."

"Thank you." She gave him a small smile. "Is that it?"

"Yes, it is." He came around his desk to walk her to the door. They stood together. The kiss in her trailer came back to him—vivid and sharp. "Are you all right?" he asked softly, knowing he was far from all right himself.

"More or less. You?" Cricket stood inches away from him, her breasts swelling and receding, inviting his touch. He could smell her skin and her shampoo, see the flecks of brown in her green irises, the velvet of her cheek.

He could see beyond her to the motivational poster beside the door, which showed a rowing team and had the ironic slogan, "Do it together and you'll do it better."

The big black-and-white clock ticked loudly in the silence. "I can't stop thinking about the other night," she said.

"Me, either." His pulse jumped...along with other parts. They were alone in the building, he knew, well after hours. Dwayne and his assistant were probably the only people on campus right now....

He could kiss her, like in that storage room. He was dying for the feel of her lips, the taste of her tongue. He could yank her into his arms and they could tumble onto the ever-wear carpet and make love, heedless of anything but each other.

She felt something similar, he could tell. She was trembling and breathing hard. She tilted her face to the side, tipped up her lips and…

"Tuck, this Dwayne." A voice called out over the intercom above their heads.

Tucker and Cricket jerked apart as if they'd been burned.

"Yes. I'm here," he called.

"Uh, if you're not too busy, could you, uh, pop on over to the gym here for a quick sec so I can show you what's what with the carpentry and locksmith issues on the stage and such?" The man couldn't say anything quickly.

"Sure, no problem," Tucker said, trying to control his breathing. "Be right there."

Cricket looked at him with dazed eyes. "Don't go."

"I have to. This is crazy, Cricket." He touched her hair, so soft. Her skin, so kissable…

"Let's go somewhere," she breathed. "There's a motel on the way to Tucson. The Hideaway. Little pink bungalows?"

"I know the place," he said, his breathing still uneven, still wanting her, despite the risk. "What if someone saw us? Even without the fake marriage, I supervise you, Cricket." But God, how he wanted to.

She snagged one of his business cards from the bookshelf by the door. "I'll call your cell when I have a room," she said, holding up his card, which contained the number.

"Don't. Really. I mean it."

"We need this. We can be discreet."

"We can't," he said.

She winked at him as she walked out the door.

Had she accepted his decision? He wasn't sure. He stood there aching for her for a few seconds, then gathered himself and headed off to talk maintenance with Dwayne.

7

DWAYNE WALKED Tucker around the stage area, droning on and on, lovingly describing each repair to the doors and locks of the prop room, mechanical room and the set storage area. He seemed to want company, but Tucker could barely think straight after what had happened with Cricket.

"All these locks need replaced," Dwayne drawled. "This here door need planing. Swolled up from the humidity."

"Sounds like we need district maintenance," Tuck said.

"Now I think I can fix some of these things myself. I just need some petty cash to buy a few parts."

"If you want that, go ahead. But put the call into district just in case, so we won't have to wait if we need them."

"I'll just see how it goes."

Next Dwayne led him around the gym, talking on and on about varnish and wood rot, and patchwork dovetails. At least the leisurely babble helped Tucker calm down about Cricket. Thank goodness he wouldn't be racing off to a no-tell motel like some adulterous husband.

Then his cell phone trilled. "Yes?" he said into it.

"Bungalow Sixteen," Cricket breathed, low and sexy.

"Oh, uh, hello, um, Forest," he said, glancing at Dwayne. "What is it?"

"Forest? Oh, I get it. You're with Dwayne still."

"Righto," he said, feeling like an idiot. *Righto?* "What can I do for you, *Forest?*"

"You can get up here now. Please. We need this. It'll make things better, I swear. And no one will know."

Tucker glanced at Dwayne, who was waiting patiently for him to end the call. Then he thought about the private room where he and Cricket could make love all night undisturbed and unseen. Miles from Copper Corners. They were both single, consenting adults, right? And maybe they did need this.

His excuses hardly mattered. Listening to Cricket's voice, hearing her need for him, he knew he wouldn't turn her down. "I'll be glad to watch the kids for you," he said on a sigh.

"Mmm And will you put me to bed, too?"

"Sure," he said with fake cheerfulness, feeling himself go red.

"And read me a bedtime story? In Braille? With your fingers? Real slow?"

He swallowed hard. "So, um, I'll come as soon as I can."

"I certainly hope you'll *come*," she breathed, weighting the word with its double meaning. "It's your turn."

"See you soon then."

"I'll be waiting. Naked."

"Good to hear it." He clicked off the phone, his hand shaking, and smiled at Dwayne.

"Everything okay? You look kind of pale."

"I'm fine. That was my, um, brother. In Tucson. I'm due over there to take care of his boys—three-year-old twins." Why was he getting so detailed?

"Nothing to be nervous about," Dwayne said, clapping him on the shoulder. "Kids are great. Just relax and play whatever games they want. You'll do fine."

Right. Playing games. That was getting to be his specialty. After a few more childcare tips, Tucker escaped from Dwayne and, an hour later, stood before a round-cornered cabin that looked like something a hobbit might live in.

It wasn't too late to back out, he knew, but the thought of Cricket on the other side of the quaintly painted door in some state of undress was too much for him to resist. He was only human, like she said. He tapped on the door.

"Password?" Cricket demanded in a low tone laced with laughter.

"Career suicide?"

She threw open the door and pulled him inside. She wore a black silk robe with a Chinese dragon embroidered above each breast. He had no doubt she was naked underneath.

He dropped his backpack, where he'd thrown a change of clothes and a toothbrush, and pulled her into his arms, burying his nose in her neck and breathing in her sweet spice. "I've been dying for you," he said.

"Me, too," she said, leaning back to look at him. "We're safe and secret and all alone. No one can bother us here."

He glanced past her and saw that the small room was as pinkly charming as her Airstream. The tiny pink desk on spindly legs held a champagne bottle in what looked like a child's sand bucket beside a small bouquet of flowers in a glass tumbler. "You bought things," he said.

"And you have too many clothes on." She nimbly unknotted his tie, whipping it off so that it whistled against his shirt before flying to the floor.

"Stop worrying," she said, starting on his buttons. "The problem is that we declared each other off-limits. That makes us irresistible. Why do you think Victorians were so hot?"

"Denial?"

"Exactly." She pushed open his shirt and spread her fingers across his chest, closing her eyes from the pleasure of it, he assumed. Her fingers felt good on him, especially when he imagined where else they would go and what else they would do. "This will be soooo good for us," she said, fumbling with his cuff buttons.

He finished the task for her, shaking his shirt to the floor. "And then we'll be back to normal?" he said, knowing how unlikely that was and not really caring, with her arms around his neck, her silk-covered breasts pressed against his chest. It would take a SWAT team and an assault vehicle to pry him away from her now.

POOR TUCKER, Cricket thought. Why did he have to give himself such a hard time about a simple sensual experience? He gripped her like he never wanted to let go, but he was still holding back.

"Just be here with me, Tucker," she whispered, rubbing at the creases in his forehead. "You're not cheating on anyone."

"Just myself," he said with a rueful smile.

"No. You're helping yourself. You're helping us both." She had to get his attention quick, before he felt too guilty and stopped altogether. So, she stepped back, untied her robe and shrugged it to the floor, inviting him to look at her. She felt a twinge of shyness, until she saw his expression—awestruck, then hungry.

He pulled her into his arms and she melted against his body, loving the way his hair-brushed chest felt against her bare breasts. He leaned down and took her mouth. The freedom of being in a private room, able to do what they wanted for as long as they wanted made the kiss rich and luxurious, slow and deep. Much better than the furtive, frantic, guilt-laden mashing they'd done so far.

Tucker lowered his hands to hold her naked bottom, sending heat and need rushing to her sex. His buckle was cold against her skin. She hated that he still wore pants.

"Get naked," she breathed and he complied, kicking off his shoes and stripping down fast.

He looked so good—muscular, but not showy—and his erection rose sturdy and demanding. And all for her.

He surprised her by lifting her into his arms. She threw her arms around his neck and enjoyed the ride for the few short steps to the bed. He meant business, she could see by the way he looked at her, and she was so glad. Desire swelled in her heart and made her ache between the legs.

He laid her on the bed—she'd already pulled back the covers—and joined her, lying beside her, one thigh between her legs.

She couldn't help a little moan of anticipation.

"I've wanted you like this since that night in your apartment six years ago," he said, cupping one breast in his hand, running his thumb slowly over the nipple, holding her gaze, making sure she liked it. "I wanted you naked and open and wanting me like this."

"I'm glad because I—oh!" She had to stop talking because he'd taken her nipple into his mouth and was sucking it in a way that sent heat in a flood through her system, which doubled when he slid one finger to the spot where she wanted him most.

She arched into his mouth and cried out. If he kept this up, she would come too quickly, and she wanted him inside her, filling her where she felt empty for him. "Be...inside me," she managed to gasp.

He released her breast. "Oh, yeah. Good idea," he murmured, smiling. He lifted himself fully over her, arms extended, keeping his weight off her. Holding her gaze, he pushed slowly into her body, pausing every few millimeters, watching her, gauging her reaction, her comfort and pleasure.

She moaned and lifted her hips to show him she wanted more.

"Oh, yeah," he said again, then pushed in deep, way deep.

"You feel so good," she said, relishing the fullness and pressure. She wrapped her legs around his waist as he pushed in and pulled out again and again, his shaft pressing against her parts in a way that sparked a keen heat. She cried out from the pleasure of it, tightened and released her hips in the effortless rhythm they found, as easy as breathing. "Oh, I'm coming," she managed to say, wanting him not to worry about her pleasure.

"Good," he said and moved faster, deeper, using perfect force. He looked into her eyes as he drove into her, searching for something, searching for her, his eyes holding a clear message: *You're mine… I'm yours.*

She loved that, wanted it, a fact that sent fear licking up and down inside her, paralleling her pleasure. What if he wanted more than she could give?

But that negative flicker was erased by the physical swell that built inside her like a surfer's most longed-for wave. Her climax whooshed through her and she shot over its curving lip.

At the same moment, Tucker spasmed inside her. She tried to focus on his release, to memorize the feeling as he gave way within her, knowing the power she had over him, needing it so she wasn't afraid of the power he had over her.

Gradually, their movements subsided, like the last laps of a retreating wave. Tucker fell to the side and pulled her onto his chest. Under her ear she heard his heart thud hard, as if trying to escape his rib cage.

He stroked her back. Their uneven breaths were a soft counterpoint in the quiet bungalow. Neither spoke. Cricket's heart was too full and her body too happy.

The moonlight gleamed on Tucker's chest. His skin was warm and elastic. Her fingers found a few drops of moisture between his pectorals. She touched her tongue to the spot. She was so grateful to feel and see and taste and smell.

"You okay?" he asked after a bit, cuddling her against him, their mingled heat and sweat and scent making a lovely cocoon.

"More than okay. If you could bottle that and sell it, we'd end war and misery forever."

Tucker slid her body up so he could kiss her. She wanted to melt into the kiss, slide over his body, make love again and again. But the intensity of her feelings scared her a little. Making love again would seem too powerful, too meaningful, right now. Like getting the lead in the play, when she'd earned just a bit part. Way too much.

It felt so big because they'd resisted so long, she was sure. Tonight was all about relieving pressure. A one-night stand to end all one-night stands. Period.

Except Tucker's penis surged against her. The hand on her back moved lower, reaching for her bottom. She knew what he had in mind and she couldn't handle it right now. She rolled away, then kissed him playfully on the nose. "How about a walk in the moonlight."

"A walk? But I do my best work lying down," he said.

"We can walk naked if you want," she murmured. "Find a big smooth rock ledge maybe…?"

They pulled on clothes—Tuck was a tad uptight for a nude stroll—and set off on the stone-lined path that led between the bungalows and up a trail among low desert hills. A light breeze carried the medicinal scent of creosote and the tang of desert dust. The crunch of their shoes on desert pebbles and a distant coyote's bark seemed loud in the quiet dark. The white moon gave the tall saguaros long, criss-crossing shadows.

As they walked, Tuck held her loosely, his arm around her waist. "I like you like this," he said, hugging her to him.

"You mean freshly laid?"

"I guess that's it. You're gentle and easy."

"As opposed to?"

"I don't know. Bristly and defensive."

"I'm only that way when you're bossy and overbearing," she said, tilting up her face to kiss his neck, feeling his pulse throb softly against her lips.

He squeezed her, laughing. "I guess this was the cure for that. I'm not bossy and you're relaxed."

"Wonder how long it will last."

"Not long enough, I'm afraid," he said, stopping and turning to face her. "I already miss you."

What if they didn't stop? She forced away that thought, knowing it was just the aftereffects of great sex and desert moonlight. "Don't say goodbye yet, Tucker. The night is young. Let's make some memories."

She grabbed his hand and tugged him toward the bungalow, loving the warmth of his fingers twined with hers. Her peace ring clicked against his wedding band, sending some kind of SOS she chose to ignore.

THERE WAS A TAP at Cricket's classroom door, then Bradford Long leaned in. "May I have a moment of your time?"

"Sure, come on in," she said, dreading another

lecture about the need for a quiet atmosphere and a neat lab. She had just a few minutes before the Ecology Club meeting would start.

"You may know that the district has urged us to engage our students in cross-curricular learning," Bradford said, sitting in a chair at her table.

"Not exactly." What the heck was he talking about?

"As department chair, Mr. Manning has asked me to implement the approach."

"Okay, what do I have to do?" She sighed. More rules.

"That's just it. Evidently, you're already incorporating it into your teaching. Mr. Manning suggested I examine your students' science projects and talk to you about them."

"The ones on the tables in the hall?"

"Yes. And I have to say that I'm impressed. The reports are thorough and fairly advanced. And each project incorporates math as well as scientific concepts, along with language arts and computer graphics."

"Why, thank you, Brad. That's a high compliment."

"I wondered if you might explain your methods to me." He cleared his throat, embarrassed, she could tell, to need her help.

She fought a grin that Dr. Science was actually asking for advice from her noisy, messy uncertified self. "I don't know that I did anything special," she said. "We talked about the subjects in class for quite a while."

Most had chosen to report on the pygmy owl or

something related to endangered species—the legal issues, environmental concerns or biological implications of extinction.

"You must have engaged in some process to lead to these results."

"Maybe it's because they felt passion for their topics."

"Passion, huh?" A smile lifted his serious mouth. "I'm not sure that's something I can engender in my students."

"Sure you can. Start a discussion about something you're passionate about." What might that be? Molecular weights? Boyle's Law? "Then see where they go from there."

"That's a possibility, I suppose."

"Hell, skip the textbook now and then, Brad. I doubt the curriculum police will track you down and shoot you."

At that very moment, Tucker appeared in her doorway, making her heart leap in her chest. "Speak of the devil."

"I'm the devil?" Tucker said. She watched him struggle to keep his face neutral when he looked at her. It had been nearly a week since the bungalow, but the mere sight of him set her nerves to twitching and her heart into overdrive. He looked like he suffered a similar torture.

"You're the curriculum cop," she said.

"I was talking with Ms. Wilde about her students' science reports, as you suggested," Bradford said.

"She's done an excellent job, hasn't she?" His eyes met hers for a quick sizzle, but he looked back at Bradford before the vibe could possibly be detected.

"Yes, she has," Bradford said, standing. "Thank you, Ms. Wilde. I'll see what I can do about eliciting some passion from my students." He smiled at her.

"Keep me posted," she said.

He left and Tucker turned to her, eyebrow lifted. "Eliciting some passion? What have you done to the man?"

She laughed, but it came out high and nervous. Tuck was standing so close she could see the little crinkles at the edges of his eyes. She loved when he popped into her room. He'd been officially observing her teaching for evaluation purposes, but she often caught a dazed expression on his face that told her he was thinking of their night together. She had the same problem. It seemed so long ago. And so fleeting.

"I told him to share something he feels passionate about with his students so they'd put more heart in their work."

"If you can get Bradford Long fired up about trying something new, you're even better than I thought."

She blushed, so pleased at his praise she didn't even try for a double entendre. For Tucker's sake, they'd been scrupulously professional at school. Tucker went overboard, she thought, treating her almost coldly when anyone else was present.

"So, I just wanted to say hello," he said softly. She could see he wanted to touch her somewhere—her cheek, her hand, her shoulder— but resisted. "I'll see you tomorrow after school for the skit rehearsal?" He sounded as hopeful as a kid. "It is on Friday, right?"

"Absolutely." She hadn't told him the whole story

about the rehearsal. He didn't know the skits were all about sex, but once he saw how good and important they were, she was certain he'd approve them for an assembly. "And the kids got parent permission, too."

"I'm glad you're being more responsible about these things," he said, all administrator.

She winced internally. Wait until he heard about the save-the-owl rally the ecology club was working on for the next zoning hearing, complete with a TV news-attracting skit. She would cross that bridge before she fell off the cliff.

"I miss you," Tuck whispered, surprising her with his boldness.

One measly night had been lighter fluid on the flame between them. Seeing the heat in his eyes now made it worse. She could hardly breathe. "I know. It seems like forever ago." Her peripheral vision caught three students meandering into the room.

"Ecology Now," she said, stepping back, breaking the spell.

"Ecology what?" Tucker said, not quite catching on.

"Club meeting," she said, tilting her head at the kids.

"Oh, of course." He cleared his throat. "I'd better get going," he said, not moving.

The kids talked in the background, while she and Tucker carried on an eloquent exchange with their eyes. *I want you… Me, too… What can we do? It's hopeless.*

Finally, reluctantly, Tucker left.

If only they had one more time together. She

would really look this time, memorize every moment, soak up the afterglow in his soft smile, store up his scent, write down every tender thing he said to her, make it be enough.

"Cricket?" one of the students called.

"Huh?" She turned to find them seated in a circle, waiting for her to join them.

"I said, for the rally skit, will you play the greedy developer?"

Oh, God. She was supposed to talk them out of the rally, not take a part in it. The student snowball was rolling on, gathering snow and momentum and trouble as it went. "I'm not sure a rally is the way to go, guys," she said. "I'm wondering about sponsoring a debate instead."

The groans of the students were so loud, they drowned out her next words.

"The Mr. Condom skit is absolutely out," Tucker said to Cricket after the student actors had left the stage —and the gym—the next afternoon.

"But it's funny and it makes important points." She faced Tucker on the empty stage, hands on her hips. The golden stage lights turned the black-painted floor between them a golden brown and made everything beyond its glow darkly empty.

At least they were no longer sitting side by side on the cafeteria bench watching the skits, their arms touching, exchanging an occasional look that hissed and sparked like a whipping power line.

"You said *role-plays*. You didn't say they were a group. With a name. And a theme. Sex, of all things."

"The Let's Talk Troupe. Isn't it perfect?"

"You should have cleared this with me, Cricket."

"That's what I'm trying to do now."

He blew out a breath. "Right, when it's too late to not disappoint the kids? Look, the idea is good. And the mock Jerry Springer skit about pregnancy is fine. It has no controversial language and it made the clear point that teen parenthood is tough."

"But we can't just scare them away from sex. We have to prepare them for it."

"With a giant condom that sounds like Barney the dinosaur? No way. The parents will go nuts. We might as well toss condoms like saltwater taffy at a parade."

"But that's the funniest one. And the kids did research about contraceptive methods and compared failure rates and side effects and everything."

"I don't want irate parents demanding my head for permitting a school-sanctioned sex club."

"You're ready to cut the heart out of a powerful, possibly life-saving educational project just because it might upset a few parents?"

"A life-saving educational project? 'Uh-yup, kids,'" he said, imitating Mr. Condom's blustery voice, "'to keep away creepy crawlies, use only condoms made of sturdy, impermeable latex, like me!'"

"Kids respond to humor."

"We're not arguing about this, Cricket. I'll have the PTA screen the skits—without Mr. Condom—and maybe the students can perform for the social relations classes."

"But that's just a handful of kids. This is vital information that all students need. You're acting like a cover-your-ass bureaucrat, Tucker, not an educational leader."

"Call me whatever you want, but do what I say."

"Come on. I know you're not that uptight." She spoke low and intimately. She hadn't exactly meant to get so personal, but it was true. Her whole body knew it. "This conservative act is so not you. Come on, Tucker…loosen up."

"This is school, Cricket. Not *that*. We can't…you can't…" He looked extremely uncomfortable. "Come here." He motioned her to the back of the stage and backed into the prop room.

She followed.

"You can't talk to me that way at school. With that tone."

"What tone? Like we're friends?"

"Like we're lovers," he said hoarsely, "and you know it."

"Okay. You're right."

"I'm your supervisor. I evaluate you, for God's sake." He ran his fingers through his hair. "We violated all the rules the other night. I take full responsibility."

"But are you sorry about it?" She hoped not. She wasn't.

"Am I…? No. God help me, no. I'm not sorry." He sagged, sliding right off his high horse. "In fact, I wish we—" His eyes sparked at her, sending a thrilling ping along her nerves. "No…forget it."

"Forget what?" she repeated. "That you wish we could do it again?"

His eyes flared *yes* like a burst of fireworks.

"We can get the same bungalow, I bet."

"That would be insane…inviting disaster." But he smiled.

"And it would be good for us, don't you think?"

"I can't stop thinking about that night," he said. The familiar heat pulsed between them in the velvety dark of the prop room. The wood, paint and linen smell of stage sets and the sweet odor of pancake makeup gave the moment the excitement of theater.

"I try to remember every detail, but it slips away," she said.

"I can't stop thinking about your mouth and how your skin feels," he said, his voice rough. "I can't stand being near you and not touching you." He pushed her hair away from her face, his fingertips brushing her skin, making her tremble. "I remember exactly how it feels to be inside you."

"You do?" she said. She placed her hands on his cheeks, loving the heat and strength she felt there, the rasp of his emerging beard. "Sometimes in class, imagine you inside me and I feel like I might pass out."

A shudder passed through him. He started to reach for her, to lean in for a kiss, but at the last minute, put his hand on the door behind her, above her head, making the door click shut. He rested his head on his arm, his eyes stormy, his expression tortured. "Not at school. That was how I got in trouble with Melissa. She reminded me of you. And now you're here for real and I want you so much." A muscle in his jaw twitched. She saw him tremble, fighting what he wanted to do, what she wanted him to do.

Every fiber in her wanted to fall into his arms, walk him back to the pile of throw rugs in the corner and make love, but she couldn't do that. Not with Tucker's conscience so raw about what happened at his other school. Not with so much at risk for him here at Copper Corners.

"We need the Hideaway, Tucker," she said. "So we can stand the torture of being at school together." They had to do something. She was ready to make love on a pile of dusty rugs or against the backdrop to *Ten Little Indians* or sitting on a three-legged bar stool in the corner. Or all three.

"It would only make things worse," he said, abruptly resolved. "We can't." He dropped his hand from the door and stepped away from her.

She hated how much more sensible he was than she. Just when she thought he was lusting out of control, he got all stern and strict and sensible. Of course, he was probably right.

He reached for the doorknob to leave. He turned it and tugged. Nothing happened. He pulled harder, bracing one foot against the doorjamb. Nothing. He banged the wall with a fist. "Damn. I thought Dwayne fixed this door."

"Evidently not. Now what?"

"We pry it open," he said. He lunged at the prop trunk, threw it open and pawed through its contents, quickly discarding a plastic bat, a foam banana and a rubber chicken. He lifted a toy rifle in triumph, but it bent on the first try.

"Could Dwayne still be on campus?" she asked.

"You want me to call Dwayne? He's no world beater, but he'll figure out what we were up to."

"Okay...I'll hide behind the costume rack and you call and say you accidentally locked yourself in here while checking the door or something."

"I guess I'd rather look like an idiot than a sex maniac." He smiled grimly, pulling out his phone. "I *am* an idiot around you." He pushed a button and listened, then shot her a thumbs-up. "Dwayne? Tucker here. Remember that sticky door to the prop room...?"

Dwayne arrived five minutes later. Cricket peeked out from between a velvet bunny suit and a plaid sports jacket and listened to Dwayne explain—in detail—why he hadn't quite worked on the door lock yet—something about parts on order—and maybe Tuck's idea about calling district maintenance would have been better.

Eventually, after a discussion about Tucker's nephews and how much cleaner the rest rooms had been lately, Dwayne left. A few seconds later, she whispered, "Is it safe?"

Tucker turned to face her in her hiding place. "As far as Dwayne, yeah. As far as us? Not at all."

She made her way through the curtain of costumes and walked up to Tucker, who looked so lost and miserable, she wanted to hold him, but she knew he wouldn't want her to.

"I have no idea what I just said to the man," Tuck continued. "I might have promised to hire his cousins to build new doors from scratch. All I could think about was touching you."

"It's a desperate feeling."

He sighed a deep, worried sigh. "Okay. One more night at the Hideaway. Just to clear our heads. And finish this."

"Sounds good." It sounded heavenly. She breathed out in tremendous relief—like a deep drink of water after a marathon run. "I'll meet you at number sixteen in ninety minutes."

"I'll be there," he said heavily, as if he were agreeing to a suicide pact. She vowed to make it worth it to him. After all, how could anything they wanted so much be bad?

8

Tucker held Cricket tight while the last tremor shook her and smiled into her hair. Pleasing her like this made him so happy. He could feel her heart thudding against his own, also thumping hard, as if they were exchanging secret messages.

It was Saturday night and Cricket had persuaded him they should spend the entire weekend together. She'd had very convincing arguments in the form of her mouth and fingers and certain whispered promises that even now sent a rush of lust through him.

He brushed her hair away from her cheek so he could run his fingers over her buttery skin. He loved holding her like this, her body relaxed, her fiery energy stilled by what they'd done. He was good for her, he believed.

"That was nice," she said, cuddling into his chest.

"Nice? That's all? I thought the earth moved."

She chuckled and propped herself up on her elbow, so that her nipple brushed his arm, sending a charge through him. He had it bad.

"Actually, the earth cracked and split and I fell to China and back," she said, running a finger in circles on his chest.

"That's what I like to hear," he said, kissing the breast that brushed his arm.

"The weekend's almost over," she said sadly. Since Friday night, they'd barely left the bed long enough to forage for food at a nearby truck stop.

"It went too fast," he said, trying to memorize the soft, sex-flushed look on her face, the tangled toss of her hair. "You're something else, you know that?"

"But what? What else am I?" she teased.

But he wanted to be serious just now. This might be his last chance. He took her hand and linked his fingers with hers, then kissed her knuckles. "You're a beautiful woman, an amazing lover and a passionate idealist."

"And a good teacher?" she asked, serious, too. "Am I good, Tucker, in your professional opinion?"

He winced at her question. It reminded him how inappropriate it was to be in bed with a teacher who worked for him. "I'll be doing a formal evaluation next month. Let's not talk about school when we're here."

"Okay, but as a friend what do you think of my teaching?"

He studied her. "As a friend?"

"And a lover," she said in a sultry tone. "It gets me so hot when you talk pedagogy."

He chuckled, loving the way she managed to joke away his guilt. She was good for him, too. "Okay, in my personal opinion, you're doing great. You have excellent rapport with your students. Your lessons show preparation. You have innovative ideas. You just need more experience and a better handle on discipline and you're on the road to being exceptional."

"But I've got a ways to go?"

"You can't expect perfection in a few weeks."

"It's because of that chemistry lab you saw me flub, isn't it? I introduced the experiment and explained the results they should get, but once they got going, I kind of got lost."

"That's normal. After you've run the same lab a few times, you'll be better able to keep things on track."

"No, it's the middle part," she said, shaking her head, falling back on the pillow in defeat. "That's my whole problem. My social work supervisor pointed that out. I like starting projects and I have great goals, but, somehow, in the middle, things fall apart."

Tucker rose on his elbow to look down at her worried face. He was touched that she'd opened herself to him. "You have something special that can't be taught, Cricket. You love the kids and you love getting them fired up about learning. Amazingly enough, some teachers don't really enjoy their students or even understand them. For them, it's more about content than kids."

"That's hard to believe."

"That's because inspiring kids is as natural to you as breathing. That's golden. And it can't be taught. That's the gift of a good teacher."

"Really?"

"Absolutely."

"Thanks," she said and her cheeks went pink. So sweet. For all that she put on a mouthy, Teflon-coated front, she was as vulnerable and tenderhearted as one of her students. "That makes me feel better."

"You should. You should feel great." A flood of emotion made him add, "I care about you."

"Thanks. I, um, care about you, too." But her body tensed and he knew they were on dangerous ground—their relationship, which had to stay sexual. "So, back to why we're here, huh? Illicit sex?" He spoke lightly, but the words came out empty of feeling.

Cricket pushed him onto his back and looked at him with surprising seriousness. "Don't guilt yourself out, Tucker," she said, misunderstanding his look. "We can handle this. This is separate from school. When you evaluate me, I'll know it's professional, not personal. And I'll be careful not to act too friendly, even when we're alone."

"Sure," he said, not entirely convinced that made it okay.

"Hell, even insanely dedicated administrators get a weekend away now and then."

"Not the married ones." He sighed. "I wish to hell I hadn't pretended to be married."

"Kinda dumb, no question. But you did it for a reason, remember? And it's only for a while. You'll be back in Phoenix in a couple of years. No harm done."

"What about you? Will you stay in Copper Corners?"

"Oh, no. It's a nice town and all. There's just not much for me here. I hardly even see my friend Mariah. If I stick with teaching, I'll need to take classes and get my credential. I'm thinking of going to California. The salaries are better and I like the state."

"That makes sense," he said. They would both move on. Except the idea made him feel hollow inside.

"I'll go to California and you'll get to work with Ben," she said. "You must be looking forward to that."

"Yeah. I feel like I owe him everything. He saw straight into me at a time when I felt like a ghost."

"You would have come around, Tucker. You're basically a straight arrow."

"I'm not so sure. Forest was away at college. My parents were obsessed with their divorce. I felt as if I was floating free and nothing mattered. Ben showed me the past didn't matter, that I could decide to change and do it. He showed me I had power over my own life."

"Oh, so *he's* the reason you're such a hard-ass now," she said, clearly trying to lighten the moment.

"Not a hard-ass. Just levelheaded. And realistic. Focused on the big picture. Aware of my potential and working toward it." And with all his heart he wanted to make Ben proud of him.

"Except you don't look like you're having much fun doing it, Tucker. I bet Ben would tell you to relax a little."

"When I relax I end up making out in an equipment room," he said. "Or spending weekends in a no-tell motel."

"Stop. We agreed this is a much-earned vacation, okay?"

"Yeah," he said. But it was still wrong. As had been his original fib about being married. The twin sins weighed on him like gravity times ten.

"When you get back to Phoenix, I bet you'll settle down, get married for real, huh?" She tapped his ring finger, the symbol of that heavy feeling.

"I'd like that."

"You look like a guy who should be married. Even though you did grab my thigh on the ladder like you meant it."

"I was preventing a fall."

"Oh, right. Safety first, huh, Tuck?"

"You got me." He smiled. "What about you? Do you see yourself settling down with someone?" He found he was holding his breath.

Her gaze, usually stubbornly confident, flickered with uncertainty before she spoke. "Maybe. It's hard to imagine being with one person for the rest of my life. How could you choose? Or ever be sure? Of yourself or the other person?"

"Lots of people do it," he said.

"And the divorce rate is fifty percent."

Her negativity irritated him. And it seemed out of character. "My brother and sister-in-law are very happy."

"I'm glad. Julie—I mean Anna—is great."

"And what about your friend Mariah? Isn't she happily married?"

"Deliriously so." She seemed to ponder that thought. "And she says Nikki's happy, too. That's Harv and Nadine's daughter."

"So, see. That's at least three happy marriages. What about your parents?"

"They're just scared to leave each other."

"Not necessarily."

"Trust me."

"The point is that lots of people make it work. And most people give it a try at least."

"I'm not like most people."

"That's true," He said, lifting his head from the pillow to look down at her. She was different from anyone he'd known or ever would know, probably. Which did something strange to his heart—a mix of longing and expected loss he didn't like one bit. Being around Cricket made him feel different—alive, on his toes, challenged. She made him think through things twice.

"I work at it. My parents were always afraid to try anything new. They live in the house my dad grew up in. Met in Chino Valley and never left. Have the same jobs they got out of high school."

"Maybe that's what they wanted."

"They're bored to death, but afraid to change. They sit in front of the TV and marvel at how scary the world is. I hate that. I swore I'd never be like them."

"You're definitely not."

"Nope. The sky's the limit for me." She looked past him, doubt skimming that sky like a cloud across her face. Then she looked back at him. "I'm surprised you're so gung ho about marriage. Didn't your parents' breakup change your ideas?"

"The problem was my parents, not marriage. They expected each other to give their lives meaning and when it didn't work that way, they harassed each other for not being enough."

"Which proves my point. My parents set their expectations too low. Yours set them too high. It's like the opening of *Anna Karenina*, 'Happy families are all alike; every unhappy family is unhappy in its own way.' And even when it works, how long can it last? Like the scientific principle of entropy, you know—everything tends to a state of lukewarm?"

"I don't buy that," he said stubbornly, his basic optimism refusing to yield to her out-of-character negativity. "If you're realistic and work at it, you can keep a marriage strong."

"You make it sound like a huge chore. Is it supposed to be that hard?"

"There has to be give and take, compromises and adjustments. Yeah, it's work. But if you love each other, it's worth it."

"Unless you're just settling, like my parents."

"I think you're giving up too easily."

They were silent for a beat of thought. Then she shot him a wicked grin—ready to change the subject, no doubt. She never liked the serious stuff. She tapped at her wrist, as if she wore a watch. "Time's a wastin'. We need to make some serious love here before you have to race home to meet your wife, jetting back from Tadjikistan."

He grimaced at the reminder of the charade he lived. "Actually, I do have to finish a grant proposal tomorrow."

"Working on Sunday? You dedicated administrators…"

"Our time's almost up," he said, not a bit ready for it.

"Of course, we could do this again next Friday…." She looked so hopeful and he was flattered that she wanted more time, but they would definitely be pushing their luck. Besides, he'd agreed to watch the twins next weekend.

"Actually, Cricket, I promised Anna and Forest I'd watch their boys next weekend."

"Oh, well." Her whole body sagged with disappointment, which made his heart ache. "This was supposed to be the end anyway." She snatched her lip between her teeth, that tender gesture that showed the vulnerability she fought to hide.

"So, why don't you come with me?"

"What?" Her eyes widened with surprise.

"You'll love the twins. And you can meet my brother and see Anna in her natural milieu."

"Oh. Wow," she said, blinking at him. He loved startling her. "But if it's a family thing…"

"It's just fun. And the boys go to bed very early, so we'll have plenty of time alone." He kissed her, giving her a sample of how it might be.

"Mmm," she said, her eyes hazy with desire. "Why not?"

For lots of reasons, he realized, even as he kissed her again. Their relationship had the life span of a small insect. And was professionally risky to boot.

But then she touched him and he was off again, riding that sea of sensual oblivion with her for as long as he could forget everything else.

"COME IN, COME IN," Anna said to Cricket at the door Saturday evening. Cricket didn't even get out *hello* before Anna had dragged her into the hallway and hugged her hard.

"Ouch." Something had stabbed her. Her good sense, maybe, since this was entirely too domestic a scene for what she and Tucker meant to each other.

"Sorry." Anna held up a rhinestone earring. "Must have poked you with the post."

"It's okay," she said, rubbing the spot.

"When Tucker told me you were coming, I was

just thrilled," Anna gushed. She hadn't even greeted Tucker, who'd gone ahead into the living room.

"Just to help with the twins," Cricket said firmly. "Tucker and I are just having fun together."

"Oh, of course. You just have all the fun you want," she said, not changing her tone a bit.

Lord.

Across the living room, a man who looked like Tucker, except shorter and broader, was making his way down the stairs, two red-haired boys clinging to his legs.

"Unca Tuck!" the thigh monkeys shrieked. They released their father and ran to Tucker, who crouched to meet them.

"Hey, guys, how's it hangin'?"

"Hangin' low," they chorused in angelic voices.

"I just cured them of saying that, Tuck," Anna said, shoving the earring into her ear and heading for the stairs. "Stewart, don't choke Unca Tuck," she said calmly. "When his face turns red that means he can't breathe."

"It's the attack of the killer nephews," Tucker said, falling over. Both giggling boys piled on top of him.

Anna paused at the foot of the stairs and turned to watch Tucker and the boys. "What a great uncle you are, Tucker," she said meaningfully, winking at Cricket before she started up the stairs.

"I'm Forest," Tuck's brother said, shaking Cricket's hand. "Don't let Anna overwhelm you."

"Nice to meet you," she said, shaking his hand. "Your boys are darling." So was Tucker. There was something really sexy about a masculine man wrestling so tenderly with little kids.

"And will you read to us, Unca Tuck?" one boy said.

"Absolutely," Tucker answered.

"And will you play hide-and-seek?" asked the other.

"You bet."

"And will you give us bad snacks?"

"Shh," he said, glancing up at Forest as if to keep the secret from their father.

"The Oreos are in the teddy bear jar," Forest said.

"Now my turn. Tickle me." One boy held up his pajama top and aimed his ribs at Tucker.

"No me," said the other, shoving his brother to the side.

Tuck tickled both and they fell to the floor again.

"I'm ready," Anna said, breezing down the stairs. When she reached Forest, she threw her arms around his neck and kissed him. "This is just like old times, huh?"

"Yeah." Forest sighed contentedly as his wife kissed his neck. Tucker hadn't exaggerated. These two were happy together.

After a flurry of exchanged phone numbers and agreements to check in and goodbye kisses and promises to "go right to sleep when Tucker and Cricket say so," Anna and Forest picked up their overnight bag and departed. They'd be back around noon the next day.

Cricket looked down at Tucker on the floor with his nephews. He seemed content and young and happy, an arm around each nephew, his hair adorably mussed. Her heart squeezed with affection. Affection and something more…the longing to be part of his life.

She tried to push out the feeling, but it swelled and lifted in her chest like a helium balloon. This was make-believe, she reminded herself. They were playing house. This wasn't what she wanted. Not for a long time anyway. Not until she felt the urge to stick around, or could hold onto her feelings longer than a few months.

Tucker was different. He was ready for this. She could see him with a couple of kids in a suburban house with a loving, stable wife. She could never see him with her.

Nor would she want to be with him. Sure, the sex was great, but he was such a bossy, controlling, buzz-kill of a guy. He'd drive her nuts.

All the same, before she knew it, she was immersed in the fun—unscrewing Oreos and adding Marshmallow Creme, crawling behind sofas to be easily found by a shiny-eyed twin, being shown toys and games the boys dragged out of their closet to impress "Auntie Cricket."

The first time Stewart—or was it Steven?—called her "auntie," Tucker had taken each boy by the hand and said soberly, "Cricket's not your auntie, pals. She's Unca Tuck's friend. Do you understand?"

"Yes!" they said in unison, then one added, "Want to see my battle copter, Auntie Cricket?"

"No, I show her battle copter," the other insisted, shoving the object into her hand.

"Sorry," Tucker said to her.

"It's okay," she said, her throat tight with unfamiliar emotions.

When every toy had been removed from the closet and lay scattered on the floor, Tucker looked at the clock. "Bedtime, pals, or your mother will never let me come watch you again."

They howled, but a bribe of extra stories soon had them cozily ensconced on the sofa, each in an adult lap. Cricket sniffed up the delicious scent of over-heated boy and baby shampoo, loving Stewart's weight, warm and trusting, on her lap. She knew the boys apart now—Stewart's face was broader than Steven's.

She read *More, More, More, Said the Baby*, complimented by Tucker for her expressiveness. He read *The Napping House*, and they read alternate pages of *When You Give A Mouse a Cookie*. The boys relaxed into the glorious hypnosis of being read to way past their bedtime.

Cricket read *I Love You Forever*, where a mother declares her love for her little boy as he grows through the stages of his life until the end of her own, when the boy-turned-man takes over the stanza about love. She finished the last line with a knot in her throat and tears in her eyes.

She closed the book, then realized both boys were asleep. When she looked up, Tucker was watching her with the most adoring look she'd ever seen.

This could be us, it said. *In love. Loving our children.*

And for just a flicker of a second, she wanted that. There must be something in the air or the baby shampoo—some insidious gas that was making her even *think* about a life like this.

"Better get these guys to bed," she said, shifting Stewart so she could stand with him in her arms.

Tucker gathered up Steven and they walked side by side up the stairs, and soon stood over the low

trundle beds and watched the little guys cuddle up
with their favorite stuffed animals—a penguin for
Stewart, a skunk for Steven—a superhero sheet
tucked under each chin. The scene was seductive, no
question. Probably a hardwired biological reaction
designed to ensure the propagation of the species.

Blech. She'd been reading too many biology texts.
She glanced at Tucker, who was looking down at the
boys with such love she could almost see his chest
swell. What a loving man he was. She tried to remember how hidebound and bossy he was, but it was impossible in the warm, sleepy room lit by golden light
made by one child-size lamp and the pale moonlight
peeking through the seascape curtains.

Tucker tilted his head toward the hall and they tiptoed out.

Cricket closed the door with a soft click. "That
was sweet."

"I'm glad you think so." There was hope in his
tone and his face, a hope that filled her with joy. And
scared her to death.

"Now it's time for some adult entertainment," she
said to get them back on track. She put her arms
around his neck and kissed him lasciviously, even
though her stomach jumped and her heart refused to
stop aching with tenderness.

Thank goodness Tucker switched into sexual
mode right away. Grabbing the baby monitor out of
the master bedroom in case the boys cried out in the
night, he joined her in the guest bed. They made love
like fiends—it had been an entire week, after all—
muffling their cries so as not to wake the boys—
rough and grabby and demanding, with nips and

bites, and her legs high over his shoulder for maximum penetration, so she could feel every inch of his thick length driving deeper into her. Damn, he was a good lover, knowing just when to speed up, when to slow down, when to deny, when to demand. For sex like this, it was worth entering dangerous domestic terrain.

After they'd fallen into a second post-orgasmic heap, Cricket rested her head on his chest and watched the moon through the open curtains. This was lovely, being with Tucker on the smallish bed. The monitor crackled and a boy's sleepy voice mumbled a word, then quieted.

"The twins are great," she murmured. "And I like your brother. He seems to adore Anna. I'm glad."

"I told you there are happy marriages." He shifted so he was looking down on her, his intensity obvious even in the dark.

"Yeah, but Anna and Forest are special people."

"So are you, Cricket. You could have a life like this." He held her gaze. This was serious.

She had to end any fantasy he might be entertaining of a future for them. "If I wanted it. I don't. Not now. Maybe not ever. This is what you want, Tucker. And I know you'll find someone who wants it, too."

He looked at her for a long, quiet moment, as her silent message sank in. "I'm just saying don't write off a life on theory," he said, masking any hurt her words had caused. He kissed her softly. "Good night, Cricket." He cozied her against him, then tugged the sheet up to carefully cover her.

She felt a little lonely now, but it was good she'd

told him how she felt. The sexual intensity between them was tough enough to keep in perspective without speculating about an impossible future.

Still, in the cozy house, with the two boys sleeping in the next room and the strong, loving man breathing under her cheek, holding onto her as if he never wanted to let her go, she could see the appeal. She could definitely see the appeal.

She'd told Tucker she wouldn't stay in Copper Corners, but she'd grown fond of the place. She loved her little trailer. She'd even grown to appreciate her nosy neighbor Mrs. Thompson, who pumped her for news, arriving with a food item in exchange—strange items suspended in Jell-O. Pistachios, sweet peas, cubes of Havarti cheese.

She liked the school, too. And teaching science, once she got the tough part down. Which she hoped would be soon.

And there was Tucker. Who had a kind, soft side that he'd shown her more and more, especially in bed. She liked his steadiness in a way. It was something solid to bounce against, ricochet away from and then return. They had similar views, after all, if he'd just loosen up a little....

Maybe she would talk to Mariah and Nikki about all this when Nikki came to town. Maybe her friends had insights about love and commitment and staying places—they'd been wild in the old days, too. But now they saw the world through the rose-colored glasses of their own happy marriages. She knew herself and her capabilities. She wasn't ready for anything serious. And no one was more serious than Tucker Manning.

As soon as he felt Cricket drop off to sleep, Tuck opened his eyes and stared at the ceiling in the dim light. With Cricket in his arms and his nephews in the next room, he was so happy. Despite Cricket's objections.

He wanted his own kids to spoil and talk to and worry about. And a wife to do all that with. He focused on Cricket's breath as it brushed his neck, watched her back rise and fall with each slow inhale and exhale.

What kind of mother would Cricket be? A fun one, who would turn the living room into an imaginary poison swamp, with the furniture the only safety or transform the backyard into an obstacle course…a creative mom, full of love and energy.

And also a pain in the ass, who would make every decision about child-rearing a power struggle—a fight about preservatives in baby food, bedtimes, how much television to watch, and on and on. Parental strife wasn't good for kids.

And she wasn't ready to settle down anyway. She opposed the idea on general principles, it seemed. Hell, she planned to go to California.

He just had all these feeling for her—as strong and unstoppable as a Mack truck going downhill. Bringing her here had distorted things, got him wishfully thinking about a life he wanted very much. Eventually. With someone.

Not Cricket. Cricket was difficult, demanding, uncooperative. Not a partner, not a team player. Except, asleep in his arms, she seemed like a perfect fit.

9

THE NEXT MORNING, Tucker awoke to find Cricket already awake playing battle copter with the twins in their room, so there was no early-morning sex. The boys kept them busy until Forest and Anna returned, but even if they'd been alone, he doubted they would have made love.

The echoes of their marriage talk had lingered and now they were awkward around each other. Cricket was polite, but distant. Why the hell had he brought it up? It had completely killed what they had.

Whatever that was.

The drive home was quiet, except for small talk. Cricket dozed. They were done, Tucker concluded. The unexpected intimacy of taking care of the twins had killed their passion like a pregnancy scare affected a pair of horny teens.

All day Monday, they avoided each other and Tucker began to feel as if someone had opened a small hole in his lungs, so he couldn't quite draw a full breath.

He headed out to his car after work. A flyer advertising a student bake sale was tucked under his wiper, but beneath it was a square envelope stapled shut in four places. His name was written on the outside in Cricket's bold, arty scrawl.

He looked around to see if anyone was nearby. No one. His heart pounded like crazy and his fingers fumbled the envelope tearing it open. Inside was a note card thanking him for his help with the Let's Talk Troupe's skits—innocent enough—but folded inside the card was a slip of paper: *I need your mouth on me. Seven p.m.*

CRICKET GASPED in relief. Whew. She and Tucker had barely made it to the squeaky pink bed before they'd climbed up and over the orgasmic peak. Absence seemed to make the heart grow hotter.

Before Tucker had arrived, Cricket had rearranged the bungalow's decent watercolors of desert plants into an attractive cluster they could see from the bed, sprayed sandalwood air freshener, lit a ylang-ylang pillar candle and covered the lamp with a red scarf to give the room a sexy glow.

"This was a bad idea, Cricket," Tucker said, clearly not meaning it.

"I know. But I was desperate."

"Me, too."

She smiled and rolled on top of him. Resting her chin on a fisted hand, she looked into his face. This was much better. The terrible settling-down thoughts she'd had at Forest and Anna's had scared her. But as soon as she got back to thinking about just sex, she'd felt a whole lot better.

And hornier.

"What are we going to do now?" he said, stroking her hair.

About us, he meant, but she wanted to stick with here and now. "How about a bubble bath?"

"I'm serious."

"Me, too. I have my best ideas in hot, soapy water."

"I'm sure you do," he said on a sigh, as if he were powerless to resist her. And she was so glad.

Ten minutes later they faced each other in the large claw-foot tub in deliciously hot water, fluffy with the Cherry Aphrodesia bath foam she'd bought for the occasion.

"Here's what I think," she said, squirting the soap bar between her hands, then slowly soaping her breasts with what remained on her fingers. Tucker watched, his mouth slightly agape. She loved how the littlest sexual thing made him wild. "I say we come out here for a few weekends."

"A few weekends?"

"Until we're done with each other."

"And how long do you think that will take?" He lifted a skeptical eyebrow.

She shrugged, not willing to think too hard about it. "A while. Or until we break the bank paying for the bungalow."

"It's risky to keep this up, Cricket."

"Not as risky as stripping each other with our eyes during faculty meetings or locking ourselves in prop closets."

"True."

"Plus, we'll be helping the entire faculty."

"How do you figure?"

"If you have some place to use up your extra energy, you won't dream up any more committees to drag people onto."

"I beg your pardon?"

"No one wants the freshman mentor thing, Tuck. Most freshmen fit in fine. The teachers find buddies for those who don't. Informally."

"I disagree. People assume things are happening that aren't."

"My point is this—a freshly laid assistant principal is a happy assistant principal." She made circles in the foam on his chest with her big toe.

"I see what you mean," he said, grasping her foot in a hot, wet palm, then splashing it clear of soap. "You have the best toes." He took her big toe between his teeth and bit gently, watching her the entire time.

"Ooh." Her eyes drifted shut with the sensation.

"And what about a freshly laid science teacher, hmm?" he asked. "Is she so relaxed and happy she won't have time to get into trouble?"

"Whatever you say," she said, loving how he was massaging her sole with both hands.

"So, I have you in my power?" He teased the space between her toes with his tongue.

"Do with me what you will," she breathed.

"Good. Because you need to tone down the diversity mural."

"What?" Her eyes flew open and her foot slid from his chest to splash in the water beside him.

"The women's chests are practically pornographic. You could plant a grove of trees in the cleavage."

"I can't tell the kids to repaint the boobs. That's their vision."

"No, that's their testosterone. At least make the nipples invisible and raise the necklines."

"You're such a puritan."

"There have been complaints."

"I'll talk to the kids. The sad part is we may not have enough paint to fix the problem."

"What do you mean?"

"We're almost out. The kids are talking about a car wash to raise some money to buy more."

"You shouldn't have to do that. I might have a budget line I can allot to it. Or...you know, I spotted a grant application from a house paint company a few weeks back. I think it was aimed at kindergarten classrooms, but maybe I can work something out."

"Really? You would do that?"

"Of course." He considered the idea for a moment. "Count on me for the paint. I'll make it happen one way or another."

"Now that's using your administrator powers for good instead of evil. Thank you."

"You've got me all wrong, Cricket."

"I certainly hope so," she said, leaning forward to kiss him, then turning her body so she lay between his legs. Water sloshed around them. She cuddled against his chest. She loved feeling his body around hers, his voice in her ear. He made her feel safe and secure, feelings she kind of liked. In small doses.

"I had one of your students in detention the other day. Jenna Garson. She was supposedly working on a report for your class, but she started throwing spitballs, tripping kids and generally messing around."

Cricket sighed. Jenna. A problem. "I'm working with her. I helped her get started on her research, but she won't take any responsibility for working on it on her own."

What was helping Jenna was the Ecology Now Club. And, worse, the rally, which was a big problem for Cricket. A problem she didn't want to ruin this moment.

"Sometimes troubled kids try to hand their lives over to you, if they see you as their savior. You need to set limits."

"I do. I am."

"I'm glad. And I wanted to tell you I'm pleased that you've cooled the owl business."

Her stomach tightened. She hadn't quite managed that. She'd told the kids that the rally, especially the skits, would entrench the opposition, but parents had gotten involved, costumes were being made, and Miriam had contacted some reporters. Plus, Jenna was alive with excitement. The other kids had asked her to play the role of the environmental activist and she was in heaven. How could she take this away from Jenna—and the other students? To protect her job? Not very honorable.

"Cricket?" Tucker said, obviously sensing her stillness. "You did cool it, right?"

"I'm in the process of," she said. She planned to suggest they do the rally at school over lunch instead of before the zoning hearing in the park across from the town hall. "Hey, we're not supposed to have school talk when we're on personal time," she said. She found Tuck's hands under the bubbles and placed them on her breasts, loving the hot, slippery feeling of his fingers on her skin.

"Good point," he said, low and hoarse, moving

against her back. She melted into him, forgetting everything but the feel of Tucker and her together in the silky, aromatic water.

Best of all, they'd have many more weekends in their little pink love nest. She'd ask the manager if she could keep the candles and bath stuff in a cupboard. This was pretty perfect. Weekends together until they were done—exciting, but safe. They were absolutely clear that their relationship had no future.

What more could she want?

"YOU WANTED TO SEE me?" Cricket asked, two weeks later, sticking her head in Tucker's office door. She sounded casual, but she was thrilled. Pretty ballsy to invite her into his office in front of God and the school secretary.

"Yes, I do. Come in, Ms. Wilde," he said in his administrator voice. Good one.

She was sure he just wanted to see her up close for a few secret minutes. He somehow managed to drop into her room every day for one thing or another. The weekends seemed so fleeting and far apart.

She shut the door behind her with a click, then pulled one of his guest chairs to the side of his desk and sat close, but not so close that anyone popping in would be suspicious.

"What did you want to see me about?" she asked, winking.

"A couple of things," he said seriously. "First, the Let's Talk Troupe."

"What would you like to know?" She spoke in a loud, fake voice, then dropped the volume to a whisper. "I miss you."

Tucker's crooked grin peeked out for a second, then he straightened his mouth. "The PTA executive committee liked all the skits, except the Mr. Condom one, as I predicted."

"That's good," she said, hardly listening to his cover story. "I can't wait to touch you." She slipped her foot out of her sandal, scooted her chair a tad closer so she could slide her toes under Tucker's pant leg.

"Cricket," he breathed, pushing his chair back and away from her.

"Yes?" she said innocently.

"The PTA is okay with the skits at an all-school assembly, as long as parents are fully informed and invited to attend with their children. And you lose the Mr. Condom one, of course."

"You're serious," she said, realizing this was a real meeting.

"Very."

She paused to clear her head. "For all students? In an assembly? Not just human relations classes?"

"As long as there's no Mr. Condom."

"What if we had him give a Surgeon General's warning thing about STDs? Throw in some scare tactics?"

"That's our offer. Take it or leave it."

She thought about it. Not too bad. Close to a complete win and next year they could try again. "It's a deal," she said, shaking his hand, loving the chance to touch him.

He held on longer than strictly necessary, his expression softening.

"Thanks for the paint, Tucker," she said. "The kids think you're a hero."

He released her hand with apparent reluctance. "So, you explained that I used my power for good, not evil?" His smile was bigger than the joke warranted, and she knew he was just so glad to see her.

She felt the same way. Just being around him for a few minutes made her feel more alive, turned colors brighter, sounds crisper, breathing sweeter. "I want you so bad I can't see straight," she said, a little scared by that fact.

"Me, too."

"I have to touch you," she said.

"Have to?"

"Yeah. It's vital." She wanted to throw herself into his lap, roll his chair against the wall and go at it. But that was impossible. "If we were alone right now, do you know what I'd do...?"

TUCKER SAT RIVETED to his chair, lust darkening his vision as Cricket described, in erotic detail, the things she'd do to him with her tongue and fingers and legs. The weekend at the bungalow seemed forever ago. Each time they made love he wanted her more. And now she was making love to him from three feet away with just words.

He looked past her, trying to focus on the ordinary things in his office—the apple plaque on the wall, the books and manuals, the birthday card from the faculty, scrawled birthday drawings from his nephews. "You've got me walking into walls," he whispered.

"I know," she said with a sigh.

"I thought we'd be less obsessed, not more."

"Who knew?"

Then he remembered worse news. "I can't come to

the Hideaway this weekend. Forest and Anna are going to Vegas for a weekend—she won a trip—so I'm watching the twins." He paused, wanting to invite Cricket to come, but knowing she wouldn't do it.

"So, let's go tonight. To make up for it."

"Tonight?" Lord, that sounded good. "It's a school night and I've got two reports to finish before tomorrow."

"So, let's get started early so we can get some sleep," she said and jumped to her feet. "I'll race you there." And she was out the door.

He sat there for a second, immobilized by his feelings for her. He'd meant to confirm that she'd told her students the demonstration was off. He'd heard kids talking about it in the lunch room. He should be exercising his authority with her. But what authority could he have over a woman who dissolved his defenses with one kiss, one touch, one look?

None whatsoever.

THE NEXT MORNING at dawn, Tucker pulled up to his house and climbed out of his Explorer, fuzzy-headed and exhausted. So much for getting some sleep. They'd had no more than a two-hour doze in there somewhere. The fact that they wouldn't be together this weekend seemed to super-fuel their lovemaking.

He started up the walk toward his house, then noticed his neighbor on his porch reading the paper. "Hey, Tucker. Late night, huh?"

"Uh, yeah."

"Watching your nephews again?" He'd excused his weekend absences as visits to his brother's place.

He gave a slight nod, hating the pile of falsehoods he lived under—an Atlas-worthy burden weighing him down.

"You're sure a great uncle," his neighbor said, shaking his head as if Tucker were crazy. Which he was. "You know, with you gone so much, your lawn's getting ragged. Flowers are drying out, too."

"I can see that." Spending every spare minute with Cricket, he barely had time to do his laundry. Forget the yard.

"I know my son would be glad to take over for you. He's got his eye on a new video game and needs to make some money."

"Um, sure. I'd appreciate that. Send him over after school and we can discuss the details."

"That way, when your wife gets back she'll have something to be proud of. I know how cranky women get when men just ignore the 'honey do' chores. When is she back again?"

"Not for a while. She's flying the Asia route these days." Lord, the neighbors were asking about Anna, who, as far as he was concerned, was on permanent foreign assignment. It was like Ben had said. Ribbed or smooth, everyone would know. What the hell was he doing?

AFTER THE LAST bell, Cricket rested her head on the stack of midterms she'd barely touched. She was exhausted from the school-night boinkathon at the Hideaway, but she couldn't leave because the ecology club would be meeting in a half hour.

The midweek visit to the bungalow had been her idea, but it had been a mistake. Maybe Tucker had a point about their affair affecting their work. She'd had to cancel noon tutoring so she could prepare for today's chemistry lab, she was hopelessly behind on her students' lab journals, and midterm grades were due tomorrow.

She'd asked her students to give themselves their own effort marks, which she would average with their midterm scores for the final grade. Except the kids had scored themselves all wrong. The highest performers were too harsh and the kids who never cracked a book too lenient. Tucker was right, this grading thing was miserable.

On top of that, the test results stank. She obviously hadn't covered the material well. Doubt seared her again. Maybe she had some good teacher traits, like Tucker had said, but she was lame with the day-to-day stuff, where the rubber met the road. Bradford had held a department meeting about state achievement tests and how they would appear on the school's public report card. That had scared her to death. Maybe she should try a different subject. Something easier—social studies or P.E. or drama or nutrition.

She sighed and tried to focus on the tests she had to score. She had to get some work done before the club meeting, which she also dreaded. She'd promised Tucker to do something about the rally.

She'd barely dug in when Bradford popped over to talk about how to use the new grading software and to thank her for her advice about the science projects, which seemed to be working for him.

Then Miriam bopped in with the owl skit scripts, followed by Leon Molroy, bubbling over about a videotape he planned as his project for Bradford's class—footage of the owls' habitat.

The kids were so jazzed about the rally. How could she cancel it? She looked up and caught sight of Jenna Garson out in the hall. The girl saw her, then frowned and rushed away.

Jenna wasn't coming to the meeting? Now that Cricket thought about it, the girl had been sullen in class that day and her report was still missing. "I'll be right back," she said to Miriam. "Don't plan anything without me." She dashed after Jenna.

AFTER THE all-nighter in the pink bungalow, Tucker had a tough time making it through the day. The final class bell rang and he shook his head to clear it. He had tons to do.

"Could I have a moment of your time?" Harvey stood in the door to his office.

"Sure." But when instead of sitting, he backed away, meaning he wanted to meet in his own office, Tucker knew Harvey was concerned about something.

He probably wanted an update on Tucker's projects. Lately, he'd seemed a little dazed by all Tucker had going on. Harvey had fought his urge to micromanage, but he liked things to be predictable.

"I've got the mentor program under control," Tucker said the instant he sat down across the desk from Harvey. "I know I said I'd have it implemented a week ago, but it's taken longer than I hoped."

"I'm not sure we need a mentor program, Tucker, but as long as you can get the volunteers, I guess there's no harm."

No harm? Hell, there were powerful benefits, according to the research, but Tucker didn't argue the point. Harvey looked gray with distress. "What's up, Harvey?"

"This is awkward, Tucker."

It must be something embarrassing. The bustlines of the women on the mural? "If it's the mural, don't worry. Cricket has promised me the kids will tone down the, um, endowments."

"That's good news. Quite the arresting features, I must say. But that's not what I want to discuss with you. The issue does concern Cricket, however."

Lord. Maybe he knew about the rally. "I've talked to her about the owl hearing and she's promised to settle the kids down."

"I appreciate that," Harvey said. "I hate to discourage a teacher with passion, but I'd like to avoid another difficult exchange with the board president, if I can."

"I'll make sure of it, Harvey. Count on me."

"I do. Very much, Tucker. And I have appreciated you working so closely with Cricket. You have a natural...rapport." He shot him a look.

Uh-oh.

"She reminds me so much of my daughter Nikki," he continued. "So delightful, so energetic. As a result, I don't have the professional dispassion I should have. Can you understand that?"

"Oh, absolutely, sir." *More than you'll ever know.*

"So I blame myself for letting things get to this point."

"Excuse me?"

Harvey cleared his throat and shifted in his seat,

the leather squeaking sharply in the quiet room, lined with bookshelves, trophies and class photos. "I know you've been assisting Cricket—evaluating her teaching, overseeing her extracurricular activities, offering her guidance. All good things. But some folks have observed that you might be a little too attentive. We're a small school, Tucker, and people talk."

"People are talking...about Cricket and me?" Dread filled him, heavy and thick as sand in his throat.

"People who like you both and are concerned for you both. It's just...I don't know how to say this." Harvey swallowed hard, his face pink. "I think the world of you, Tucker. And your wife is a dear woman—so supportive. But with her away so much of the time, it would be easy for Cricket to be, well, a distraction. We're all human. And she's a remarkable woman."

Tucker felt his face flame so hot with guilt he probably glowed. He opened his mouth to say something, anything, but Harvey held up his hand.

"Now I know you would never jeopardize your marriage or hurt your sweet wife. But for the sake of appearances, I think you should be careful—above reproach, you know?"

"Of course," he said faintly.

"Cricket doesn't need more trouble. She's raised some eyebrows already with her environmental activities and that acting group and such. I'd like to see us protect her."

"You're absolutely right, sir. I feel the same way."

"Just bear in mind what I have said."

"I will, sir." He felt sick at heart that Harvey was worried about him. *I know you would never jeopardize your marriage.* Harvey trusted him. And he'd violated that trust from the moment the man had offered him the job.

"I'm glad you understand," Harvey said, jovial with relief. "You know the old saying—opportunity knocks, but temptation leans on the bell."

"I never heard that one." The urge to confess rose in him. How could he hold onto the lie when Harvey was looking out for him—and Cricket—this way? He felt like a weak jerk.

He walked out of Harvey's office, shaky and ashamed. In some ways, this was worse than getting caught making out by the volleyball girls. This was a warning he and Cricket had to heed. Thinking hard, he walked out of the building onto the quad.

He would definitely stay away from her at school—no more meetings in his office, no more observing skit practices just to be with her. No more dropping by her room to say hello. But that wasn't enough and he knew it.

He had to stop seeing her. The thought made him physically ill. He had to tell her, talk to her about what Harvey had said, but he didn't dare go to her room. He'd call her at home tonight.

He was looking at her building, longing to talk to her, when he saw two students head inside hauling fake-fur suits and bizarre headpieces sporting big eyes. Owl eyes. That meant only one thing. The rally was still on. Now he *had* to talk to Cricket. And it wouldn't be pleasant.

She wasn't in her classroom room, however,

though students were—passing out stapled papers and talking intently. A cardboard cutout of a bulldozer rested against Cricket's desk. "Where is Ms. Wilde?" he asked a student hammering a hand-lettered sign—*We Speak for the Pygmies*—onto a stake.

"She's down the hall," the student said.

"Talking to Jenna Garson," a girl added.

He remembered their bathtub conversation about Jenna. Cricket was probably setting the limits they'd discussed. She was doing her best to be a good teacher. She wasn't used to disappointing students, after all, which happened to every teacher from time to time. He could see the kids were excited. Maybe he could help her, save her some agony.

"Students," he said loudly. "May I have your attention?"

"Shut up, guys," someone yelled. "Mr. Manning wants to talk."

10

CRICKET WATCHED Jenna clump away from their conversation, tempted to go after her, but the Ecology Now kids were waiting. Jenna had been hurt when Cricket hadn't shown up in the library yesterday to help her—she'd been with Tucker. She hadn't promised to be there, but she understood how Jenna might count on that.

She'd let Jenna down, which made the bungalow visit seem even worse. Even her offer to go over Jenna's rough draft hadn't eased the girl's hurt.

Now she had to return to the club and disappoint more students. The hallway seemed like a long tunnel, echoing with the click of her heels. The scent of books, old wood and chemicals from the lab—the smells that had excited her the first weeks of school—now made the air seem thick and hard to breathe. She felt trapped. What was she doing here? It seemed all wrong, scary, impossibly hard. Fighting the urge to just keep walking, she took a deep breath and crossed the threshold into her classroom.

Tucker stood at the end of the table speaking to the students, who were silent, though their misery-filled faces told her that whatever he was saying they didn't like.

"Mr. Manning says we can't do the rally," Jason announced.

"You what?" she asked Tucker.

"I told them it's not your fault—it's district policy." His expression warned her not to argue with him.

"What if we do it anyway?" Jason demanded of Tucker.

"That would be unfortunate," he said calmly, "since I have instructed you not to do so."

"But we can act as individuals, right? Not as a school club. You can't stop us from going to a public meeting."

A few students murmured agreement.

"But what about Cricket?" Miriam said. "Will Cricket get in trouble if we do the rally?"

"As I said, faculty members have to be careful about their involvement in controversial political activities." He gave Cricket a pointed look. Was he threatening her? Frustration bubbled up and she fought the urge to object.

"Mr. Harvey and I want Ms. Wilde to have a good year so she can keep teaching here," he continued to the students. "We value her as much as you do. If you want to help her, you'll cancel the rally."

"You expect us to sit back and do nothing?" Miriam demanded.

"Send a representative to the hearing with the petition signatures you've gathered, as I suggested."

"But no rally, no skit and no speeches," Jason said.

"Exactly."

Everyone groaned. Feet shuffled, palms and pencils hit the table in an angry staccato.

"Again, this is not Ms. Wilde's fault," Tucker said, surprisingly unaffected by the students' anger, which would have upset Cricket terribly. "She didn't realize how serious this could be. One of the hard truths about the world is that there are risks to some things we do. But there's almost always a safe way to accomplish what we want. Like your petitions, for example. That is a valuable effort."

Cricket stared at him. She knew he was trying to help. He was taking the blame so she wouldn't have to. But she didn't appreciate his assumption that she couldn't do this herself. She'd planned to. And she would have, too. As much as she dreaded it.

"I'll let you talk it over with your teacher," he said. "And, once again, Mr. Winfield and I are proud of you for working to support something you believe in. We just ask that you use good judgment. For everyone's sake."

Tucker gave her a look that he probably meant to be kind, but came across as smug, then left. She watched him go, irritation and gratitude warring inside her.

"We don't want you to get fired," Miriam said. Sad faces around the table nodded solemn agreement. "So, I guess we can do what Mr. Manning said. Maybe my dad can get the attorney to speak at the hearing."

Deflated sighs filled the room. She couldn't stand how heartbroken they were. It was her fault, no matter what Tucker said.

"What about my videotape?" Leon Molroy said. "Can I still run my videotape? It shows how they could build around the actual cactus where the birds are. Make a park, kind of, you know?"

"Of course you can show your video," Cricket said. "Absolutely. I'll call the commission and arrange for a VCR to be at the hearing."

"My dad should call," Miriam said. "You might get in trouble."

"For asking to show a video? That's ridiculous."

"We don't want you to lose your job," Miriam repeated. "You can't take chances."

They talked about a few options, but the silences between comments grew long and heavy, so the students gathered their things and left. Cricket felt helpless. She hadn't been able to give them hope or even help them accept this failure.

Tucker's appearance had thrown her, caught her off guard. He'd taken over her job. She would talk to him about that.

She walked straight into Tucker's open office and shut the door behind her. "I want to talk about what just happened," she said.

"I saw the kids with costumes going into your room, so I knew you hadn't canceled the rally. I figured you didn't want to disappoint the students, so I helped you out."

His intentions were good, she knew, but something about his father-knows-best tone bothered her. "You took over without asking me."

"I know. But now they can be angry at me and not you."

"But it was my job to do."

"You're right," he said with a sigh that was heavy with sadness. "And if I'd been doing my job, I would have reprimanded you for not canceling the rally. But I didn't. I couldn't. Because we're together." He looked so troubled, she knew there was more both-ering him.

"What's wrong, Tucker?"

"We need to talk. Sit down." He indicated the chair beside his desk.

She sat, her heart thudding in her chest. "What happened?"

"Harvey called me into his office this afternoon," he said, looking into her eyes. "He wanted to warn me that people think I'm spending too much time with you."

"He did? Does he know?" Fear rushed through her at the possibility.

"No. He's worried about our reputations, though. He's grateful that I've 'helped' you so much." He used finger quotes around *helped*. "He also said he knows I would never hurt Julie, but he's afraid I'll be tempted by you…because you're so remarkable."

"Oh, no. I'm so sorry." Poor Tucker, having to face Harvey's innocent concern, knowing the entire time how much worse things really were.

"It's my fault, Cricket. The man trusted me. He's looking out for both of us, while I've been lying through my teeth to him." Tucker looked positively eaten up with guilt, his eyes bloodshot and sad.

"It's not just you. It was my idea we sleep to-gether." They looked at each other, guilt passing be-tween them in a slow wave. "So, what should we do?" Then she answered her own question. "We have to stop."

He nodded. "I don't want to make the lie worse than it already is."

"You're right."

They looked at each other for a long, lonely moment. "I should go," Cricket said finally. "We shouldn't be alone together with the door shut." She smiled sadly and stood.

He nodded and walked her to the door.

She turned to him and felt something that surprised her—relief. What was that about? The situation was impossible, maybe, and it was better to end it before anyone got hurt? Before Tucker got hurt. Cricket's feelings never lasted.

He stood very close to her now, his eyes sparking with regret and heat. "Too bad we couldn't have one last time," he said, hope in his voice.

"Someone could see us."

"Of all the times for you to be the sensible one," he said, stroking her cheek.

"It had to happen sometime." His touch sent desire hurtling through her, erasing her relief, making her yearn for more time, making her want to take back her words, to figure some way to make it work. "So this is goodbye," she said, trembling to her toes.

"Yes." His voice was hoarse with need.

"Okay, then." She fought the longing to wrap her arms around him and kiss them both mindless.

"Right. It's over."

"Exactly."

They met in a kiss so hard their teeth clacked, grabbing at each other desperately, until they somehow managed to break apart.

"Okay...that's it," she said dazedly. "Absolutely the end."

"Right," he said, breathing hard. "We're finished."

She turned the knob on his office door to leave, her

mind spinning, her body protesting, her heart thudding desperately in her chest.

"Cricket?"

She turned back, ready to throw herself into Tucker's arms, forget the risk, go for broke. Except he looked at her dead on, all business. "You'll make sure the students cancel the rally, right?"

She felt stung. She still reeled with lust and yearning, but Vice Principal Manning was back to following school rules. "Yes, I will," she said. "Just don't tell me it's for my own good."

THAT SATURDAY, Tucker stood in the living room of his brother's house and held open his arms to his nephews barreling straight for him. Just before they reached him, they stopped dead. "Where's Auntie Cricket?" Steven asked.

Stewart looked past Tuck, as if she might be hiding behind him.

"You didn't bring her?" Anna had come down the stairs and sounded as disappointed as the twins.

"She was busy this weekend," he said, still crouched at the boys' level.

"But I want her," Stewart said. "She made bad snacks."

"I have to show her my tower," Steven said.

"Hey, there. Unca Tuck will make snacks and look at your tower."

They looked at him soberly. He was definitely second-string now.

"What did you do, Tucker?" Anna said, her hands on her hips. "Did you piss her off?"

"We agreed to stop seeing each other." The words

sounded lonely and cold. "It's too risky. Harvey had a heart-to-heart with me about how I might be tempted with my you-know-who off flying so much." He tilted his head at the boys.

"Guys, why don't you go get books for Unca Tuck?" Anna said, evidently trying to get rid of them.

The twins headed off, disappointment in their posture and pace.

"He suspects you and Cricket?" Anna said.

"It's worse. He's worried about our reputations. I should never have done this fake marriage thing."

"It was our best thinking at the time, Tucker," she said. "We didn't know it would get complicated. We didn't know you'd fall in love."

"I'm not in love."

"Oh, please." She rolled her eyes. "Look, I could run off with my copilot so you could get divorced and then—"

"No more plots, Anna. This is over."

"You can't give up now." Anna put a hand on his shoulder in uncharacteristic sympathy. "You're miserable, Tuck. You look like someone died."

"Who died?" Forest asked, coming down the stairs with a suitcase.

"No one yet, but Tucker's high on my list," Anna said. "He's just giving up on Cricket."

"Don't give up, Tuck," Forest said. "When you find the woman you want, you have to do what it takes to get her."

He looked from his brother to Anna, their expressions identical. They were absolutely certain about something he was completely confused about. "Even if I wanted more with her, even if I could somehow come clean at Copper Corners, Cricket doesn't want me."

She'd had relief written all over her face when they agreed to end it. *Relief.* Lust, too, of course, but she wanted out. And that had stung.

Without him realizing, thoughts of a future with Cricket had trickled into his awareness, eroded his resistance, so that he'd had the urge to march into Harvey's office and confess it all, damn the consequences, make it work somehow. She'd obviously had none of those thoughts. He felt like a fool.

So he'd said something lame—ordered her to be sure the rally was canceled. She hadn't liked that, but it had given him the distance he needed.

"She's just scared," Anna said. "Every woman, no matter how tough and confident she seems, gets scared about falling in love. Have you told her how you feel?"

"I don't know how I feel. Exactly."

"Oh, for God's sake. You're in love with her, you big dope. Don't you know that? Tell her."

"Even if I am, so what? We're not a good match. We're heading in different directions. She's right to want out."

"Do I have to call her?"

"God, no. No more help from you, please, Anna."

"She won't help anymore," Forest said firmly. "This is for Tucker to sort out. Go get your cosmetics packed so we can get going." He patted Anna on the rear as she reluctantly left.

Forest looked at him with kindness. "Talk to Cricket, bro. I can only hold Anna back so long, you know."

"I don't know if I want that, Forest," he said. And he didn't. What made him think he wanted more? Her energy, her attitude, her openness? Definitely those traits. She woke him up, kept him on his toes. She was fun and creative and fresh. But also stubborn and unrealistic and critical of anything that smacked of a rule or requirement. Maybe it was just how good they were in bed together. Maybe he'd confused lust with love. In the ordinary day-to-day, Cricket would drive him crazy.

Wouldn't she?

The boys trailed into the room, each carrying a book. "Well, here are my book boys," he said cheerfully. He plopped onto the sofa and patted a cushion on either side. Steven and Stewart crawled into place and Stewart dropped his book on Tuck's lap. It was *I Love You Forever*, the story Cricket had gotten teary over. He began reading, but he had to clear his throat every few lines.

A few pages in, Stewart sighed and took the book away from him. "Auntie Cricket reads more better. Bring her over, okay?"

Tucker's heart squeezed like a fist. "I don't know, sport."

What if Anna was right and he did love her? And maybe she loved him, but she was just scared. He should talk to her about it. What was the worst that could happen? She'd tell him he was nuts, his pride would be damaged, but he'd get over it, and they'd move on. At least he would know.

But if they loved each other, if they wanted to be together...what the hell would he do then?

"Are you gonna read, Unca Tuck?" Steven asked.

He looked at the book Steven had placed on his lap. *The Little Engine Who Could.* Perfect.

CRICKET SAW MARIAH and Nikki sitting near the stage in Louie's Italian Restaurant. That was because Nathan, Mariah's husband, would be playing sax later. She took a deep breath and headed their way. She'd decided to fight her misery and avoid all mention of Tucker. The situation was impossible, after all, and she didn't dare let Nikki know she'd had a thing with someone at her father's school.

"Hey, girls!" she said, so happy to see them that her loneliness faded for a moment.

"Cricket!" Nikki and Mariah jumped up and took turns hugging her. There were a few minutes of mutual admiration over hair and clothes, Nikki's fabulous after-baby figure and Mariah's two-year-old daughter's exploits, then all three sat so that Nikki could show Cricket photos of the baby boy now being doted over by Grammie and Grampie Winfield. Nikki and Mariah had spent most of the previous day together, so this was familiar ground for Mariah.

The joy in the photos of Nikki and her family glowed so bright it almost hurt Cricket to see it. "I'm so happy for you, Nik," she said, hugging her with one arm.

"Me, too," Mariah said. "You did good."

"So, how are you adjusting to this gopher hole of a town, Cricket?" Nikki asked, putting the photos back in her wallet with a happy sigh.

"Hey, I happen to love this gopher hole of a town," Mariah said.

"You've been blinded by happiness—and Nathan."

"I like it here," Cricket said. "Everyone's friendly." Whenever she pulled into her trailer court, she felt the warmth of home. She'd even begun to voluntarily submit to Mrs. Thompson's social probes, bringing her a tossed green salad to counteract the bizarre Jell-O combos, but Mrs. Thompson had sadly refused—fresh greens gave her and Mr. T. gas. Cricket told Nikki and Mariah all about that—and about Nikki's mom wooing her with leftovers and friendly concern.

"Don't you feel smothered?" Nikki probed.

"Not really." She kind of liked it. It made her feel comfortable, valued, part of things. Kind of strange to realize she'd missed that aspect of small-town life during the years she'd been away from Chino Valley.

"Hmm." Nikki squinted at her, scrutinizing her face, and the area above her head. "Something's up. Your aura's shaky—a mix of gray and red, with sparks of gold." Nikki, who had psychic tendencies, ran a New Age tattoo parlor, where she chose tattoos based on the auras of her clients. Kooky, but people found her insights uncanny.

Nikki had hidden her career from Nadine and Harvey for years, until the truth came out during a visit home with her fiancé-to-be. That was a great story Nikki had shared with her when she'd called about a possible teaching job at her father's school.

"It's probably because of work," Cricket said. She babbled a bit about curriculum and exams and student problems, until Nikki interrupted.

"Uh-uh. This is a love thing."

"I love teaching?" she tried lamely.

"Maybe she just needs to get laid," Mariah said. "You should drop by the factory, Cricket. We've got some stud muffins in the shipping room. They load a couple crates of prickly pear jam on their shoulders and mmm-mmm-mmm, muscle central."

Nikki slugged Mariah. "You're married, girl."

"Can't I live vicariously through my single friends?"

"So, you think Cricket can fall in love with the nearest well-hung worker?"

"She doesn't have to find a soul mate to enjoy the machinery."

"Is that how it started with Nathan—just the machinery?"

"Of course not. Though falling into that vat of jelly did speed things along."

"A vat of jelly? What was that about?" Cricket asked, glad of the distraction from her own catastrophe.

Mariah recounted the story of a tumble into a stainless steel drum on the candy-making floor and the jelly wrestling match that made Mariah and Nathan say "uncle" to love.

"That sounds crazy," Cricket said. "In a good way."

"It was. And I'm still crazy—about him," Mariah said on a sigh, looking at the stage, where a dark-haired man with a gleaming saxophone was moving to sit on a stool. He blew Mariah a kiss and smiled at Cricket and Nikki. Light glinted off a diamond in his earlobe.

"I love that stud," Nikki mused.

"Hands off. You have your own stud," Mariah said.

"In his ear, silly."

"Oh, right. I had to make him a kamikaze and promise another motorcycle camping trip, but he likes it now. He just has to get used to these things."

"I wish I could get Hollis to show you his new tattoo," Nikki said. "It's a little smiling molar on his left butt cheek."

"Because he's a dentist?" Cricket asked.

"Yes. It's the most cunning design—classy, even. But he'll never show my friends, not even as a professional courtesy."

"These things take time," Mariah said.

"Anyway, no more stalling, Cricket," Nikki said, leaning closer, her chin on her fist. "What's the love trouble you're in?"

"No trouble," she said faintly, Nikki knowing would be a disaster. After finally telling her parents the truth about her own life, Nikki was an all-truth, all-the-time girl.

"Mariah?" Nikki said. "Shall we?"

"Tequila, you think?" Mariah said, like a doctor on a consult.

Nikki nodded and raised her hand to catch the waiter's attention.

Cricket's friends plied her with prickly pear margaritas—the mix from Mariah's candy factory—until she finally confessed about Tucker. Afterward, she grabbed Nikki by both forearms. "Promise you won't say a word to your father."

"It's your story to tell," Nikki said. "But I swear my father will understand. He seems hopelessly fossilized, but he's not that bad anymore. Hollis and I helped him open up."

"There's no point in telling him because there's nothing to tell." Cricket said. "We're too different."

"Different is good," Nikki said. "Different means friction and friction means sparks and sparks mean fire. All good. Way good. Trust me on this."

"Not in this case. He's such an *administrator*—Mr. Rule Book. I'm open. He's uptight. He's got a career path. He wants to settle down and have kids. I'm not even close."

"We see what you mean." Nikki and Mariah looked at each other and smiled.

"You do?"

"Oh, yeah," Mariah said. "You're perfect for each other."

Something about her expression made Cricket's two friends burst out laughing.

"Oh, sweetie, you are *so* hooked," Nikki said.

"I am not," she said grumpily.

"He'll come around," Nikki said. "If I can get a tattoo on Hollister Marx's butt and Mariah can get boring old Nathan to play sax in a bar, not to mention wear an earring, you can loosen up Assistant Principal Do-Right."

"Look, even if I could get him to change, there's the fact that he's married, plus, here's the real deal, how long will I want to be with him anyway?"

"Forever," they both said at once, her own personal Greek chorus telling her precisely what she did not want to hear…or dare to believe.

CRICKET HURRIED DOWN the corridor, running late for first hour. She'd thought about the Tucker situation all day Sunday. What if they did have the good kind of friction? Could Tucker change? Loosen up? Would her feelings stay strong? It seemed so impossible. She wasn't like Mariah and Nikki, was she?

Rounding the corner to her classroom, she saw Jenna Garson waiting for her. "Cricket!" she said, her face bright and excited. Gone was the betrayed look from the other day and Cricket was so relieved.

As soon as she reached Jenna, the girl thrust a bright yellow flyer into her hand. "Save the Pygmy Owl" was the headline and it announced the rally. At the bottom was a disclaimer: "Independent student action...in no way affiliated with Copper Corners High or any program or teacher at Copper Corners High."

"It was my idea to put 'independent student action' on there. And I got the flyers printed myself."

"You did?" Lord. What could she say now that wouldn't crush the girl's spirit? "But Mr. Manning told us to cancel. I promised him I'd make sure."

"This is a new rally. And we left you out of it." She was so proud and happy and confident. What now? The students were risking trouble for themselves, but trying to keep her safe.

"You could get in trouble, too, Jenna. You could get suspended from school."

"We don't care. Like you said, if activists backed down every time they got threatened, change would never happen."

She had said that. And she was so glad to see Jenna standing proud, her shoulders back, fire in her eyes. She felt like a coward in the face of Jenna's courage—Jenna and the rest of her students. What kind of example was she setting, cowering in the corner, hiding behind her job, while they spoke out for what they believed in?

She didn't have time to debate this further—with Jenna or herself. Class was about to start. "Thanks for telling me, Jenna," she said and folded the flyer into her purse.

As soon as classes ended for the day, Cricket headed to Tucker's office to talk to him about the rally—and beg him not to punish the students.

He welcomed her in. "I was just going to call you in," he said, an oddly tender smile on his face. He shut the door.

"Should we be alone with the door shut?" she asked.

"The twins missed you, Cricket," he said, looking positively dreamy—entirely out of character.

"They did?" The thought of those sweet guys started an ache in her chest, momentarily distracting her from her mission.

"I'm definitely second-rate with them now. You're number one."

"That's nice," she said, touched that the boys remembered her so fondly. "Tucker, listen, I need to talk to you about this." She took the folded flyer out of her purse and handed it to him.

He didn't even look at it. "They wouldn't let me read the book you read to them. They want you to do it."

"That's nice," she said, confused, her heart beating crazily in her chest at the look on his face. "Read this." She unfolded the flyer and waved it under his nose.

"I think I'm in love with you, Cricket," he said.

"You're what? You're… Oh." She felt like she'd been punched in the stomach. She couldn't draw a clear breath.

"So, what do you think?" he said.

Tucker loved her. He *loved* her. Joy rushed through her…followed by panic. Did she love him? If she did, how long would it last? She was in over her head—just like in chemistry lab…only worse. "I don't know," she said. "I mean, how can you…? We're so different. And you're supposed to be married."

"I know," he said. "It's crazy. But if we want to be together…if we love each other…" He paused, looking hopeful and young and so full of emotion, waiting, she knew, for her to speak.

I love you, too. She wanted to say that. So much. But she was afraid, too. Afraid that it wouldn't last, that it wasn't real. So she said, "The kids are holding the rally."

"What?" He looked puzzled, then startled.

She lifted his hand—the one holding the flyer—so the yellow paper was in front of his face. He read it, then glared at her. "You promised me you'd stop this."

"I tried. They're doing it without me."

"You expect me to believe that? That you didn't know about this?"

"Yes. You think I would lie to you?"

"I don't know what you'd do, Cricket. I just told you I'm in love with you and you wave this in my face." He crumpled the flyer and tossed it past her into the trash can. "I don't understand you."

And she knew it was true. He didn't understand

her and he never would. In the face of that, love
hardly mattered. Or it certainly wouldn't for long.
"No, you don't. You don't understand me. And I
don't understand you, either."

"What do you want from me, Cricket?" She could
see the hurt in his eyes, but she had to push on—for
both their sakes. He meant in a relationship, but she
focused on school.

"I want you to not punish these kids for acting on
their beliefs. Please. Just look the other way. For them."

He stared at her for a long, silent moment. She
watched the love fade to resignation. "I'll do what I
can," he said tiredly. "I don't want students to suffer
because of your bad judgment."

"Thank you, Tucker."

"You'd better not be at the rally, Cricket," he said
fiercely. "If you are, I'll have no choice but to discipline you."

"Discipline me? For supporting my students?"

"For deliberately disobeying a direct instruction. At
the very least, I'll have to put a letter of reprimand in
your file. Depending on how the board reacts, it might
have to be a suspension. Don't push this, Cricket." His
eyes were dark with emotion. "Don't risk your job just
to make me the enemy—to wreck what's between us."

"What's between us to wreck? Sex? Wishful thinking? You're in love with love, Tucker, not me."

And then she had to get out of there, escape from
Tucker and how he made her feel—scared and angry
and lost and in love.

Maybe he was a little right. And she had to get
away from that, too.

11

IN THE END, CRICKET went to the rally. She had to. She had to guide the students, keep their comments reasonable and ensure school officials weren't blamed for the event. That seemed the most responsible thing to do.

Tucker would discipline her. She would deal with that. She had to support her students, show respect for their commitment.

She wouldn't let herself think about the hint of truth in Tucker's words—that she might welcome this as a way to put distance between them.

Now that she was here, she knew it was the right thing to do. She was so proud of her students. The skit over, they clumsily bowed in their bulky costumes on the makeshift stage of picnic tables shoved together. A pink-and-purple sunset served as a dramatic backdrop as Jenna vowed to speak out for creatures who could not speak out for themselves, her voice ringing out, strong and clear.

For that alone, it was worth it. To see Jenna blossom and mature. To see her students take action to support their beliefs. No matter what happened to Cricket afterward, she wouldn't regret this.

Applause and cheers filled the air from dozens of

students and parents in the audience. Cameras flashed and television cameras rolled tape—three crews had come all the way from Phoenix. The zoning meeting would begin in a few minutes across the street from the park where they stood.

As Cricket applauded, she noticed her fingertips were black with the spray paint she'd used touching up the cardboard bulldozer right before the rally. She was glad she'd been able to help a little.

"Excuse me, Ms. Wilde?"

She turned to find a television reporter, cameraman at his side, holding a microphone under his chin. "We understand you're responsible for organizing this protest." He extended the mic to her.

She took a deep breath. Here was her chance to put the situation in the best light. "No. The kids made this happen. All on their own."

"But you sponsor the club that arranged this, correct?"

"I sponsor the Ecology Now Club. But this is an independent rally, which the school does not endorse." There. The official disclaimer was on the record. She could only hope it made airtime.

"But you do agree with what the students are saying? You believe the development should be stopped?"

She looked at the reporter steadily. She could equivocate. She could evade. But her students were counting on her. "Yes," she said firmly. "My students have presented their research to me and it's convincing. I believe in their cause."

"Thank you," the reporter said. "That's it," he said to the cameraman, who pushed a button and removed the camera from his shoulder. The reporter confirmed the spelling of her name and left. When she looked up, Tucker was headed her way, his expression stony, his mouth hard.

When he reached her, he spoke without smiling, his eyes angry and cold. "Be in my office at seven-thirty tomorrow morning. Bring your union rep—Bradford, I believe. Listen to him, if you won't listen to me. He'll give you good advice." He paused and his face softened for a moment. "It didn't have to be this way."

"I don't know any other way to be," she said.

His face resumed its harsh expression and without another word, he walked away, his posture tight with anger.

Another reporter approached—this one with a notepad. Cricket answered her questions, then led her to Miriam, the student spokesperson.

By the time Cricket made her way into the hearing room, the place was packed. People stood along the aisles and across the back of the room, where Cricket took a spot, nervous and hopeful.

The head commissioner gaveled the meeting to order. "We understand most of you are here because of the Bluestone Development project," he said. "For that reason, we'll suspend the reading of the minutes and other agenda items and begin with a limited amount of public comment on that issue."

The kids cheered.

The commissioner slammed down his gavel. "You will remain orderly or you will be asked to leave."

The kids grumbled into silence.

Alternating pro and con, the commissioners called

on speakers for three-minute statements. On her turn, Miriam spoke passionately and presented the stacks of signed petitions to huge applause. The developers offered a PowerPoint presentation on the economic value of the development, after which an environmental expert Miriam's father had located demanded time for a more thorough environmental survey of the site.

When the Bluestone Development attorney got up to speak, Cricket was startled to realize he was the president of the school board, which helped explain why Tucker and Harvey had wanted her to stop the protest. He read from a report that claimed the owls actually inhabited cactus that were a half mile from the housing site and would not be harmed by the construction. She knew that Leon Molroy's video footage proved that wasn't true.

Four more students were waiting to speak when the head commissioner declared an end to comments. The amplified pounding of his gavel overrode the students' cries of dismay. The commission would take its vote after other business was concluded.

Puzzled by the delay, the students became restless. Time passed. Tedious issues were discussed at length. Eight o'clock went by, then nine, then ten. Cricket feared that holding off the vote was a ploy to thin the anti-Bluestone crowd. As the room emptied, Cricket's sense of dread increased.

By midnight, when the vote was taken, only a few stalwart Ecology Now members remained. To Cricket's alarm and the shocked gasps of the students, the vote was four to one against them. Construction would continue and the saguaros that served as the remaining habitat for the pygmy owls would be removed. They had lost.

When the meeting ended, reporters rushed to talk to the students, who crowded around Cricket, angry and disillusioned. "What are we going to do?" Miriam asked, her eyes desperate for some hope.

"I'm not sure," Cricket said. She'd spent so much time worrying about the rally, she hadn't given a thought to dealing with a no vote. It hadn't seemed possible.

"You said if we made our voices heard, we could stop them," Jenna said bitterly. Her face was blotched with red. She'd taken this very badly.

"I thought we could. But sometimes…things don't go like we want them to," Cricket said. So lame.

"We worked so hard. We presented our case. We were right," Miriam said, her voice going high. "How did we lose?"

"It's a shock, I know," Cricket said. "What about legal action? Miriam, what did your father's attorney friend say?"

"That it will cost thousands just to get the guy to file the papers. There's a retainer and fees and all."

"We could have a car wash or a bake sale," someone suggested.

"Do you have any idea how many cars we'd have to wash to make a thousand K?" Jason said.

"I didn't get to show my video," Leon said. "With the idea about the park."

"Perhaps we can find an attorney through the Sierra Club who might take the case pro bono," Cricket said, floundering for any reassuring thought.

"Forget it," another student said, disgust in his

voice. "We lost. The owls lost. The little guy always loses."

"This sucks," said another. There was a chorus of agreement.

After a few beats of silence, Jason said, "We could stage a protest at the site—chain ourselves to the bulldozers."

"No," Cricket said. "Extreme actions won't help. We'll figure out something." That sounded hopeless even to her.

"We have to stop them," Jenna said, so fiercely that everyone turned to her. "They can't do it. They can't kill the owls." Her pale and angry face said it all.

Afterward, Cricket headed home, troubled and heartsick. For one fleeting moment, she wished she could meet Tucker at the Hideaway, rest her head on his chest and let him give her his know-it-all advice. Instead, he'd give her some kind of reprimand tomorrow in his office. She deserved it, but not for the reasons he'd give. She should have prepared the kids for a no vote. Had a backup plan. Somehow softened the blow.

She turned into Friendly Wheels Trailer Village and headed for her lovely Airstream, cold comfort after what had just happened. Her headlights flashed on the silver side of her trailer, then revealed someone standing on her porch, blocking his eyes from the glare of her beams.

It was Tucker. Out in the open for God and Mrs. Thompson to see. Cricket stopped her car and rushed up to him, so relieved she felt tears swell in her eyes.

He didn't speak, just pulled her into his arms, burying his face in her hair.

She wanted to stand there forever, but she had to protect him. "Let's get inside." Once in the door, she said, "What are you doing here?"

"I've been walking around for hours thinking about things—the rally and you and me," he said. "I looked up and realized I was standing at the entrance to your trailer park and knew I had to see you." He looked closely at her. "You've been crying."

"They voted against us, Tucker. Four to one. They're destroying the habitat."

"I'm sorry," he said.

"The kids are devastated." A tear slid over Cricket's lid and down her cheek. "I didn't know what to say to them. I tried to give them hope, but it all sounded so lame."

"Kids are resilient," he said, brushing the tear from her cheek. "They bounce back." He pulled her into his arms. "I should have stayed for the hearing—been there to help you." He leaned back to look at her face. "I was angry at you for personal reasons, and I let you down."

"You did what you thought was right," she said.

He looked so humble and so concerned that her heart throbbed with tenderness and…love. She did love him. She knew that now. She opened her mouth to say so, but he spoke first.

"You were right about us, Cricket. We're different people going in different directions. Maybe you remind me of how I used to be—open and impulsive and idealistic. Maybe I miss that about myself. I know you don't want what I want—a family, settling down, all that." He studied her face, resigned and sad.

"Tucker, I don't know what to say." Even as he said how different they were, she realized she liked that fact. She liked his steadiness and predictability, even valued it. The very moment Cricket was ready to go for it, give love a try, Tucker had given up. Maybe he loved her, but not enough.

"You're a remarkable woman, Cricket, so I guess I can be forgiven for falling for you. But I can't forgive myself for failing you."

"Failing me?" An ache swelled inside her until she wanted to curl into a ball and cry her eyes out. "You didn't fail me."

"As your supervisor, I did. I should have insisted you stop this rally before it went this far. And, when I failed at that, I should have been at the meeting, mitigated things, protected you and the students."

"You couldn't have stopped me, Tucker." She tried to smile, fighting the urge to cry. "No one could."

"Maybe not." He smiled, too. "You're one stubborn woman. But I let my personal feelings for you interfere with my job—a mistake I made before—and now I've let you and your students get caught in the middle. I'm so sorry."

"No, I'm the one who's sorry." Sorry that so much separated them. Sorry that she'd been right to hold back. She put her arms around him and buried her face in his neck to hide how sad she was.

"You feel so good in my arms," he said in her ear, gripping her as if his life depended on it.

She squeezed her eyes shut, reveling in the familiar heat that rose between them. Their bodies fit so well together, felt so right….

And then he kissed her. How could he not? "It can

be our goodbye," he whispered and leaned back to look at her.

"Yes," she said, knowing he wanted to make love. "One last time."

He lifted her into his arms and carried her to her bedroom, as he had that first time in the bungalow, holding her gaze as tightly as his arms gripped her legs.

They made love slowly and wordlessly, letting eyes and mouths and bodies say everything. Love, possession, desperation, all of it was there with them in her bed. *I want you… Don't forget me… You'll be with me always.*

The moonlight shimmered on the curves of Tuck's body and in his eyes, which gleamed with an extra light. With each thrust, Cricket felt him give more of himself to her. With each lift of her hips, she offered more of herself to him.

In the warm dark, it was okay to love him. This was goodbye, after all. She fell asleep lying on his chest, knowing he would sneak away before dawn and when she awoke it would be as if he'd never been there at all.

TUCKER FELT CRICKET drift off to sleep, her cheek on his chest. He breathed deeply of her vanilla-cinnamon smell, trying to store it up for later. Even as he'd said it was over, his love for her had expanded in his heart like air in his lungs.

He'd lied about that—to himself as well as her. It wasn't just that she reminded him of who he once was. He loved her. The way she was. As herself. But that would never work. He had a path to travel, a path that led away from Cricket.

He gently slid out from under her and stood, looking down at her, peaceful in sleep. How he loved her. He'd wanted to hang onto her, hold her, like a firefly in a jar, to sparkle and gleam for him alone. But Cricket would not be trapped or held. Even if she'd considered the idea, agreed to try it, it would never work. Their differences were too big, just as she'd said.

The fingernails curled by her cheek were outlined in black paint—probably from working on the diversity mural. He smiled. Cricket threw herself into everything she did. She'd thrown herself into him, too. But that was over. All over.

He turned and left her bedroom. He had to get to school early to prepare for the fallout from the student rally. Maybe it wouldn't be too bad, since the commission had decided against the students. He'd shield Cricket as much as he could from criticism, take responsibility for letting things go as far as they had.

He tiptoed out and closed the door of the Airstream with a soft click, shutting himself off from Cricket and all they'd shared. He half expected to see Mrs. Thompson and her Pekingese, didn't care nearly enough about the danger of being spotted.

But there was no one, and he knew that when he drove away, it would be as if he'd never been here at all.

CRICKET WOKE WITH a heart as empty as her bed and tried to be strong. She'd get over this. She'd gotten through relationships before. Though none had ever felt like this, like her insides were hollow as the Tin

Man's chest, echoing and achy. She sat up, shook her head and tried to focus on what she faced—a discipline meeting with Tucker at seven-thirty and a day of buoying her heartbroken students. How she dreaded it.

When her shower didn't remove a bit of the black paint on her fingers, she stopped at Mrs. Thompson's for some turpentine before going to school. No sense looking like a derelict.

Cricket was surprised to see a sheriff's car parked in the school's parking lot when she arrived. Students were gathered by the front door, including Miriam and Jeff, who looked worried.

Catching sight of her, they hurried her way. "You won't believe this," Jason said. "Someone set one of the framed-out houses at Copper Basin on fire."

"You're kidding."

"They sprayed 'Pygmy owls rule' on the walls of one and set another on fire," Miriam added. "Burned a bunch of it down."

"They'll find a way to blame it on the club, I know," Jason said.

"We were all pretty upset at the meeting," Miriam said. They stared at each other for a long moment. "Especially Jenna."

"Yeah," Jason said, "she was insanely pissed."

"She's always pissed about something," Miriam said. But they all three looked at each other with anxious doubts.

Cricket remembered how ferocious the girl's face had been. *We have to stop them,* she'd said. Surely, she wouldn't do something so extreme. Cricket's stomach knotted.

Cricket hurried inside and the secretary ushered her into Harvey's office, where the sheriff stood talking to Harvey and Tuck.

"The sheriff believes a Copper Corners High student vandalized the Copper Basin site," Tuck said to her.

"Why do they think that?" she said.

"There were clues." Tucker tried to reassure her with his eyes, but she could tell he was worried. "The stub of a school pencil."

"And this." The sheriff held up a plastic bag, which contained a spray-paint can. The same brand as the ones Tucker had gotten donated for the mural.

"A pencil and spray paint. How is that proof?"

"They can get fingerprints, Cricket. And a saliva sample from some sunflower seeds found at the scene."

"Sunflower seeds?" Jenna was forever chewing the things in class, leaving a little pile of hulls on the floor under her desk. Cricket sank into the nearest chair.

"We'll want to talk to all the kids who were at the zoning hearing," the sheriff was saying. "I'll need a list from you."

"I can't believe any of my students would do this." She looked up at Tucker, stricken with guilt and worry.

"If they did, you had no way to know, Cricket," Tucker said firmly.

A few hours later, Cricket watched, chilled to her soul, as Jenna Garson was placed into the back seat of the sheriff's car. She'd confessed after a few tough questions. As the car drove away, she glared out the window straight at Cricket. She undoubtedly thought Cricket had turned her in.

She had to talk to the girl—her parents, too—sort this out. Surely the authorities would be lenient with her. She was so young. She'd acted in anger and panic.

What had happened to Jenna was terrible enough, but Cricket had more bad news. After school let out, Harvey called her to his office. She figured it was about her involvement in the rally—the letter of reprimand—but she was surprised Harvey, not Tucker, would meet with her.

But it wasn't about the rally. The sheriff wanted to talk to her. Jenna had accused Cricket of helping her plan and carry out the vandalism. As insane as that seemed, there was evidence. They'd already questioned Cricket's neighbors about her whereabouts and Mrs. Thompson had reported that she'd had black spray paint on her fingers this morning. *Thank you, Mrs. Thompson.*

Jenna also claimed that Cricket had helped her find eco-terrorist sites on the Internet and suggested "subversive" readings. It was true that a list of suggested books had included *The Monkey Wrench Gang*, a sixties novel about disrupting the destruction of wilderness, but the accusation was ridiculous. And she'd helped Jenna do research for her report, not teach her how to vandalize property.

She tried to explain to the sheriff that Jenna was striking out in panic. Somehow, she must have thought Cricket wanted her to do this terrible thing or blamed her for getting caught. The sheriff listened, his face a stone mask, and then he asked her, "Where were you last night between midnight and 3:00 a.m., Ms. Wilde?"

"At home. I went straight home after the commission hearing." Straight home and into Tucker's arms.

"Can anyone corroborate that fact?"

Tucker could, because she'd slept on his chest. But if he did, the truth would come out about their affair. And that was impossible.

"No," she said. "No one."

The sheriff told her they would search the library computers she'd used, acting as though that fact might make her confess. He suggested that maybe she'd hinted at the vandalism or used examples that Jenna might have interpreted as instructions.

His words were ugly and Cricket grew angrier and angrier...which made her sound guiltier and guiltier. In the end, the sheriff sent her home and told her not to talk to anyone about the situation. She would hear from him soon.

Harvey tried to reassure her, walking her to the door. "Don't you worry. Tucker and I will be in touch." As she started across the parking lot, Tucker ran out to her.

"What happened?"

"It's terrible. I'm not supposed to talk about it," she said, fighting tears. "Talk to Harvey."

"I'll call you," he said firmly.

She drove home, shaking and scared, hardly able to breathe. She felt more alone and lost than she'd ever felt in her life. And guilty. So guilty. How had she missed the signs of trouble with Jenna?

She couldn't wait to get home to cry and think. But when she pulled into her carport, there was Mrs. Thompson running up the walk, two bowls of Jell-O jiggling in her arms—one yellow, one blue.

"I hope I didn't cause you any trouble by talking to the deputy," she said, hardly allowing Cricket to climb out of her car before rattling on, "I knew it wasn't anything, but the truth is always best, isn't it? I told them the paint was from the rally, but they just jumped to conclusions."

"Sure," Cricket said, accepting the bowls of apology Jell-O. "And you didn't need to make me anything." *Besides a suspect*, but she kept that ironic observation to herself.

"I knew you'd be too upset to fix anything," she said. "And I think what you're doing about the owls is a good thing. Mr. T. and I are always for the underdog…or underbird, I guess, in this case."

"I appreciate that, Mrs. Thompson, but I need to get inside." She was desperate to cry in peace and talk to Tucker when he called. She set the Jell-O bowls on the counter, when she got inside. The yellow one seemed to contain thin pieces of beef, while the blue held jelly beans and marshmallows. Dinner and dessert, no doubt.

The message light was blinking on her phone machine. She rushed to pick up Tucker's message. Instead, a woman's hateful growl emerged: "How dare you brainwash our girl with your garbage? You've ruined us. We'll sue you into the ground, so help me God!" The woman—Jenna's mother—called Cricket ugly names, her voice going high and fierce until she abruptly hung up. With a mother so full of rage, no wonder Jenna was troubled.

The phone rang and Cricket jumped. Still shaking from the hate-filled message, at first she couldn't speak.

"Cricket? Are you there?" Tucker. Thank God.

"I'm so glad it's you." She clung to the phone as if it were a lifeline. Harvey had filled Tuck in on Jenna's accusations and he reassured her as best he could.

"It's ridiculous to even consider that you were involved," he said. "I'll tell them I was with you and end this."

"You can't."

"I have to."

Her heart squeezed at his willingness to give up his secret to protect her. "I'm sure Jenna will tell the truth when they pressure her. She's probably just terrified of her mother."

"I won't let you suffer for this, Cricket. You've already got too much to deal with."

Something in his tone caught her. "What else do I have to deal with?"

He paused. "No matter what, Cricket, remember that you are a good teacher. Don't you dare lose faith in yourself."

"What's the matter? What are you trying to tell me?"

"You've been put on administrative leave."

"I've what?"

"You'll be paid, of course, but the district thinks you should be out of the classroom until this is settled."

"You mean Harvey thinks I did something wrong?"

"No. Harvey's worried about you. It's the school board president. The newspaper coverage made the kids out to be heroes, which embarrassed the hell out

of him. You're quoted, too, as supporting the kids.
There is a suspicion that you incited Jenna's actions.
And her parents have demanded you be fired. But
don't worry. We'll straighten this out at your hearing."

"My hearing? You mean I could lose my job?"

Tucker paused and she knew the answer before he
spoke. "I know it's unfair, but people are scared.
Nothing like this has ever happened in Copper Corners. They're afraid of the idea that a teacher could
urge students to do something like Jenna did."

"They think I could do that?" She sank onto the
sofa, the phone clutched to her ear, her stomach roil-
ing, her heart pounding against her rib cage. Fear
and anger filled her mind.

"You'll be exonerated. Don't worry. By the time
I'm finished, they'll name you Teacher of the Year."

"I don't believe it, Tucker."

"I know. I blame myself. I'm sure Harvey does,
too."

"It wasn't your fault. I was too stubborn to listen."

She'd been too stubborn about everything. And
now she would pay.

12

THE DAYS BEFORE her school-board hearing were a roller coaster for Cricket. The phone rang often—mostly students, parents and colleagues offering encouragement and support. But there were a few anonymous hate calls. Mrs. Thompson came over daily for coffee and some of the Jell-O Cricket didn't have the appetite to eat. *Shame for it to go to waste*, her neighbor always said with a shake of her head, as she scooped out a blob or two.

Tucker called every day to give her a pep talk and make sure she was keeping busy. He was determined to make things right and his calm confidence boosted her spirits. She longed to fall into his comforting arms, but he didn't dare come to her house. More and more, she valued his stable, steady, careful presence in her life.

One afternoon, the Ecology Now kids arrived to present her with impassioned letters and flowers. They wanted to come to the hearing to defend her, but Tucker had convinced them it would look like Cricket had orchestrated their attendance.

At first she was furious about her plight. How dare the school board assume the worst about her and her students? She couldn't wait to tell them exactly what she thought of their narrow-minded ignorance.

But as her hearing approached, her doubts increased. She'd let the club go too far. A student who'd looked up to her had been arrested doing something she somehow thought Cricket wanted her to do. Cricket *had* encouraged her students to take action without fully considering consequences. Maybe she'd inadvertently incited the vandalism.

She'd been in over her head for sure. Tucker had told her to focus on teaching, but she'd ignored him. Jumped ahead to the results, forgetting all the teaching and guidance she was supposed to give along the way. And look what had resulted.

She'd been so concerned about her mission and her integrity she'd ignored the implications. Maybe the school board was right to ask her to defend herself.

TUCKER SAT AT HIS desk Wednesday afternoon looking over his notes. Cricket's hearing was tonight in the gym and he was as prepared as he could be and completely determined. There was no way he would allow the board to fire Cricket. He would resign first. It was his fault, not hers. He'd allowed an enthusiastic new teacher to put herself in harm's way.

His door opened and Harvey came in and dropped into his guest chair. "Are we set for tonight?" he asked. Harvey was as committed as Tucker was to making sure Cricket kept her job. He'd had one-on-one talks with each board member, but it would be a close vote. The board president had a lot of influence. "Absolutely," Tucker said. "I've got supportive letters from faculty, parents and students. Even Dwayne wrote a note about the lack of trash in the bathrooms and graffiti on campus. The kids are too busy with Cricket's activities to get into mischief. He calls it The Cricket Effect."

Harvey smiled. "Kind of a stretch, don't you think?"

"Dwayne just wants to help. He's fond of her."

"We all are. She's quite a gal, isn't she?"

"Yes, she is." And he loved her desperately. He cleared his throat and continued explaining the plan. "Bradford will speak as her union rep and department chair. He has some anecdotes he wants to share about her influence on his own teaching."

"Sounds good."

"Then I'll share my formal evaluation of her teaching. And I'll talk about my failure to set clear limits." He paused, then looked directly at Harvey. "I screwed up. I know it."

"We learn these things the hard way, Tucker. I blame myself for leaving the situation too much in your hands. There's a middle ground between hands-off and handcuffs that I need to identify."

"It was my fault, Harvey. I know that and I'm taking full responsibility." His mistakes and the reason for them—his personal feelings for Cricket— haunted him night and day. "Then you can make any closing remarks you'd like to."

"Sounds like a plan, Tucker."

"Great." They looked at each other for a moment. "From now on, I'll keep you in the loop all the way. I know you trusted me, Harvey, and maybe I haven't lived up to that trust." He didn't want to say more.

"When it's convenient, I'd like to talk about how I can do a better job."

Harvey looked uncomfortable. "Maybe we should talk now."

"If you want to," he said, puzzled by the suggestion, especially right before Cricket's hearing. "Well, I thought next year we might consider going to a bloc schedule—the research says that ninety-minute periods are more conducive to learning. I've done some preliminary schedules and I think—"

Harvey interrupted, "So, you plan to stay next year?"

"Yes, of course. Why do you ask?"

"I know you said you wanted to return to Phoenix. I wondered if you were considering it for next year."

"No."

Harvey had turned pink and he was blinking rapidly.

"Is something wrong?"

"I'm in a bit of a quandary, Tucker, you see, and it would work out well if you wanted to move on. I can promise a great recommendation."

"You want me to leave?" He couldn't believe it.

"Truth is, I'm looking for a successor, Tuck. Nadine would like to travel and we'd both like to see more of our grandson in Phoenix. So, I'd like someone in place who could take over for me when I retire."

"And you don't see me as that person?"

"You're dedicated and conscientious and knowledgeable, Tucker, but you're obviously working toward something bigger and more interesting than Copper Corners."

"More interesting?"

"I know you're bored. You've started project after project."

"You think I started projects out of boredom?"

Harvey gave him a long look. "Why else? We certainly don't need extra clubs or triplicate forms. And the extra committees make the faculty cranky."

"Why didn't you say something?"

"I wanted you to be autonomous, as we discussed. Hands-off and all that. I would have had to say something next year, but, well, the thing is that I've been approached by a former Copper Corners graduate, newly certified as an administrator, who would love to come home—raise his family here."

"And you want to hire him?"

"His résumé is attractive. He loves it here."

"But I've enjoyed working with you, Harvey," he said. More than he'd even realized until the man suggested he leave. He hadn't thought about Western Sun in a long time.

"And I you. I don't have a son, Tucker, and, well, I can be forgiven for some fatherly feelings, can't I?"

"I'm honored." His throat was tight with emotion.

"You belong in a larger school environment. Not everyone's cut out for a small school."

He felt the floor tilt under him. He thought he'd been doing a great job, but Harvey wanted him gone.

"And living in a city might be better for you…on a personal level." He looked uncomfortable. "With Anna gone so much, you must be quite lonely."

Oh, lord.

"I don't want to pry, Tucker, but is everything all right…at home?"

"At home? Fine," he said, swallowing hard. "Just fine." His mind spun with this new conversational twist. Harvey had announced he was failing at his job and now he'd brought up Tucker's fake marriage, a source of deep guilt.

"Everyone struggles from time to time," Harvey said. "There's no shame in that. No need to put up a front. The truth is always easier to take than a lie when it comes out."

"You're right about that." Harvey was giving him a perfect opening to confess about Anna, but he was too stunned to say anything.

"You know, our daughter Nikki told us some whoppers a while back..." Harvey went into a story about his daughter pretending to be married to a doctor and owning a boutique that was really a tattoo parlor, but Tucker could hardly focus. He needed to think, to sort out what to do, and Cricket's job was on the line in a meeting a mere hour away.

"And now she and her husband are very happy," Harvey concluded. "And we're close as a family for the first time in forever. Nadine and I learned to let people be who they are. That's my advice to you, Tucker, about your work. Be who you truly are where you truly want to be."

"I appreciate your concern, Harvey. And your advice."

Basically, he'd failed at the very things he thought were his strengths—his new programs, his fresh ideas. Instead, he'd overdone everything, made the staff cranky and made Harvey long for a replacement. On top of that, Harvey had basically invited

Tucker to admit that he and Anna were having marital problems.

"So, what do you say, Tuck? Shall I write you a recommendation letter, make some calls?"

Tucker looked into the concerned face of his principal—a man he admired, a man he'd lied to from the moment he'd said yes to the job. Harvey was handing Tucker exactly what he wanted—a recommendation—earlier than he'd planned even. He could say yes and call Ben, see about teaching at Western Sun for the two years until the assistant principal spot came open again. But right now all he felt was confused and misunderstood and, dammit, hurt.

"Can I take some time to decide?"

"Sure." He patted Tucker's shoulder. "Take all the time you need. Just let me know by next Friday, when Roger—the man I was telling you about—stops in."

CRICKET CLIMBED OUT of her car in the parking lot the night of her hearing, her nervous jitters contrasting with the soft air and comfortable dusk.

The parking lot was jammed with cars and there were two television trucks. This would be a circus. The idea knotted her stomach. She could only pray her students had obeyed Tucker and not come.

She hugged herself with clammy hands and her heart fluttered in her chest like a trapped bird as she headed for the auditorium door. She saw that Tucker stood on the steps waiting for her. Just looking at him made her feel better.

When she reached him, he said, "It will be all right. We'll give 'em hell, don't you worry." But he looked shaky—as if he were worried, too.

"You've done too much for me already, Tucker," she said. "You have to protect your job, too."

"My job? I haven't been handling that as well as I should," he said. Where was his confidence? Had she done that to him? How could she have been so selfish? Barreling ahead with her plan, ignoring the negatives for her kids and even Tucker, who was new here, too. She's gotten him in trouble, as well as herself.

Tucker kept trying to cheer her, but she couldn't avoid the fact that she'd brought this entire disaster on herself—on him, on the school, the community and, worst of all, on her students.

In that moment, she knew what she had to do. The idea had flitted through her brain during the week she'd been on leave, but she'd shoved it away, focusing instead on her outrage.

Now that didn't seem important. "Thank you for all you've done for me," she said and squeezed his forearm. "It means more than I can say." She released him and walked on toward the front of the room.

The cafeteria benches were full of people. The few students sat with their parents, thank goodness, so Cricket couldn't be blamed for their presence. As she passed, she accepted smiles and raised fists and up-thrust thumbs and ignored the few glares and frowns. Jenna's mother was there, staring stonily ahead, her mouth a bitter twist.

Near the stage, the board was seated at a long table—four men and a woman, their faces serious, reading over papers. Bradford stood in the aisle, tall and straight, smiling warmly at her, waiting. He'd been wise and calm during their consultations, bringing baked goods from his wife, which she'd barely been able to taste. Bradford was a sweet, good-hearted man and a damned good teacher, she'd come to realize, in his own way. They'd learned from each other.

He helped her into a chair beside him, with Harvey on her other side. Harvey smiled at her. Tucker joined them, sitting on Harvey's far side.

The board president called the meeting to order, then invited Bradford to speak.

But Cricket put her hand on Bradford's arm. "I'd like to speak first," she said and stood, her knees shaking despite her confidence that this was the right thing to do.

"Go ahead," the board president said, looking grim.

"First, I want to say that I appreciate all the help I've received from everyone." She motioned at the men sitting beside her. "And especially my students—" she looked out at the audience "—who have supported me all along. But now it's time for me to support them."

The room went still as the audience seemed to hold its collective breath.

"I want to make it clear that I had nothing to do with vandalizing the damaged houses. I urged my students to look into the issue, to gather evidence and speak out on behalf of something they believed in. That was the right thing to do."

Some of the audience clapped.

"But I was still wrong."

Bradford stood. "Cricket, don't," he said. He was obviously afraid she'd ruin his defense. But that was the last of her concerns right now.

"It's okay, Brad," she said, motioning him down. "I was wrong because I got carried away with ideals and ignored reality, even when Mr. Manning, my administrator, repeatedly warned me of the danger. You were right, Tucker." She smiled at him, but his worried face made her want to cry, so she looked away and blinked. She had to stay strong. She cleared her throat.

"Let me be clear. Mr. Manning specifically told me to stop the rally. I defied him. He suggested positive alternatives. I ignored them. Tucker Manning is guilty of one thing only—giving an eager new teacher the chance to make mistakes. He should be honored for that, not condemned. I know he'll try to take the blame for me, but I can't allow that."

"Cricket," Tucker rose. "Please don't do this."

"I have to. I owe you an apology. And Harvey, too. But most of all," she turned to the audience, "I owe you, my students, an apology. I wanted the best for you, but I didn't provide it. I didn't prepare you. I didn't help you when the chips were down. I'm especially sorry for what I did to Jenna Garson. I wasn't there for Jenna, and I regret that terribly."

Through blurred eyes, she saw that Miriam was crying.

Then she turned to face the board. "I made a serious mistake. I hurt a lot of people. For that reason, I ask you to accept my resignation from my position as science teacher at Copper Corners High."

The audience rumbled and gasped. A voice yelled, "No!"

Bradford and Tucker were on their feet again.

The board president called for order. "Ms. Wilde, take a minute to consult with your representative."

"I've made my decision. This is best for everyone. I've broken your trust and let everyone down. You need a teacher who knows what she's doing. I wasn't ready for this responsibility. But I promise you I've learned my lesson. I'll learn more about teaching before I try it again. I'll never forget the people here or my students, but for everyone's sake, I need to leave."

Her throat was so tight she knew she'd cry any minute. "Thank you," she said and, biting her lip to hold back her tears, she turned to walk as fast as she could down the aisle and out the door. Behind her, she heard the roar of people talking over each other.

Once outside, she began to run, feeling free and scared and sad. She started for her car, but her gaze snagged on the school. She wanted to see her classroom again. To say goodbye to what she'd tried to do there.

She set off across the desert landscaping, tears streaming unheeded down her cheeks. This was best. She would start over somewhere else. She'd get her credential, for sure. Maybe work as an aide or school secretary in the meantime so she could stay in education. Tucker was right—teaching was a chance to influence the next generation. Teaching touched the future.

"MR. PRESIDENT, may I please speak?" Tucker said, but he didn't wait for permission. He'd speak if he had to shout the board president down—or punch him in the face. "I must strenuously urge the board to refuse Ms. Wilde's resignation."

His loud announcement quieted the crowd.

"Go ahead, Mr. Manning," the board president said.

"Cricket Wilde is the kind of teacher every parent wants for their child. She's caring, committed, supportive, full of ideas and enthusiasm. She has infused this school with energy and life. Our custodian spends the afternoon reading mysteries in the lounge because the bathrooms and hallways and walls are clean—our students are too busy with Ms. Wilde's activities to get into trouble. We call it 'The Cricket Effect.' You should be giving her an award, not making her defend herself."

He turned to gesture at the audience. "Look at the students who are here. These aren't the apathetic kids we see everywhere, focused only on the next mindless movie, nihilistic pop song or senselessly violent video game. They care. They took action in a cause they saw as just. They did that because Cricket showed them how."

He turned back to the board. "Maybe Ms. Wilde, in her inexperience, missed some clues that might have prevented the destruction that occurred, but I know she never, ever encouraged such acts. I was very close to Ms. Wilde."

This was the hard part, but it was the first step to making everything right again. His chance and Cricket's chance for a fresh start.

"If any of you still doubt her innocence, I must tell you that I know where Cricket was the night of the fire."

"Tucker," Bradford hissed from beside him. "Don't do this."

"Because I was with her," he said, ignoring the

warning. "In her home. I was there to say goodbye, to end our relationship. I was in love with her, you see. In fact, I still am."

A gasp rose from the crowd.

"I am not married. This is fake." He held up his hand and pointed at the ring, still a heavy weight on his hand, but feeling lighter by the second. "When Harvey Winfield offered me this job, he had the impression I was married and I thought it was better for Copper Corners if I let him go on believing that. Somehow, I forgot that being honest with yourself is the first rule of success."

He paused, surveyed the board, who were blinking in shock, but listening to every word. "I thought a lot of things would be good for Copper Corners High that weren't. Harvey set me straight this afternoon." He looked down at the man, who seemed completely stunned. "You asked me if I was ready to move to a bigger district, Harvey. The answer is no. What I'd like to do is start over here. Apply for my job again, as the man I am, as a man who will listen to what you and the staff want, what the students need, instead of doing what I think everyone should want and need."

Harvey cleared his throat, gathered himself, and stood. "I'd like to talk with you about that, Tucker," he said, his eyes lit with what looked like relief. "Tomorrow morning, if you'd like."

"Thank you," he said. He had a chance. That was all he needed. He turned back to the board. "So, again, I ask you to refuse Cricket Wilde's resignation. I don't intend to let her quit on me. Don't let her quit on us. Or the kids of Copper Corners."

The room erupted in applause and cheers. And for the first time in five months, Tucker felt free. The Atlas-worthy weight of guilt lifted from him and he took a deep fresh breath. The first since the mistake at Western Sun. From now on, he'd be who he truly was, not who he thought he had to be to prove himself worthy of Ben Alton's rescue or pride. He would do the work he loved where he loved it—right here in Copper Corners.

And the person he had to tell all this to was Cricket.

First, though, he had to find her.

THE FIRST THING Cricket saw once she reached the campus quad was a butcher paper banner strung across the breezeway that said, *Free the Owl Avenger. Support Ms. Wilde.* Posters dotted the walls of her building. As she neared, she could read their slogans: "Free Ms. Wilde"…"Good teachers: An Endangered Species"…"We love Ms. Wilde, the heart of our school." She had to blink hard at the sight.

Inside Building D, she paused to look at the nearly finished mural, which showed diversity, community, compassion and love—and all without supersized boobs. She smiled, then continued down the hall, breathing in the familiar scent of lab chemicals and books and paper and Magic Markers. The scent of school.

God, she'd missed this in the week she'd been gone. Maybe she would teach science after all in California—after she had all the teaching methods classes she needed, of course.

At her classroom door, her heart squeezed with

anticipation. She opened the door, flipped on the light and stepped inside, flooded with happiness. She loved this room. The animals in the terrarium, the papier-mâché trees—reports pinned to its limbs—the bulletin boards filled with artwork and essays. She loved everything she'd accomplished here.

Her desk was piled with papers. Essays, it looked like, assigned by her sub—the school secretary. The top one was titled "How Ms. Wilde stood up for us" and was written by a student who rarely spoke in class.

Then she spotted a stack of magenta flyers on her desk. They advertised a "Car Wash for Freedom" to raise money for her defense.

The VCR cart had been pushed into the middle of the room. An empty tape box rested on top. It was labeled "The Ferruginous Pygmy Owl—Fierce Fighter Faces Destruction" in felt marker, followed by Leon Molroy's name.

The developers should see this tape, she remembered. Leon had laid out a clear case for a park for the owls. She could envision her students presenting the tape to the developers—bearding the lion in his den. She'd have to make sure the kids knew it was a long shot, so they wouldn't be devastated if it failed, but they had public sentiment on their side, and a park could be a face-saving move for the developers.

But that was a job for another teacher—her replacement. But who would they hire who would care enough? Perhaps she could stay long enough to see that through....

"Ms. Wilde?"

She turned and saw Jenna Garson standing a few feet inside her door, her arms wrapped tightly around herself.

"Jenna! Come in." She motioned at her.

Jenna didn't move. "You can't quit," she blurted angrily, tears in her eyes. "I was in the car and saw you come out. My mom told me you quit. You can't quit. Everyone will blame me."

"It's not your fault," Cricket said. "I was wrong. I didn't give you enough guidance, Jenna."

"So tell them you're sorry and stay."

"I can't." She swallowed hard. "What's going to happen with your case?"

"The developers don't want publicity, my lawyer says, so my parents just have to pay for the damage, and I have to do community service. But I want to move. I'm begging my parents to move to California."

"The kids understand why you did what you did. They were angry, too. You can get through this. I know you can."

"So can you."

"It's different for me." Cricket's mind whirled. Was it? Was it really different? Jenna wanted to run from her mistake. Was that what Cricket was doing?

"I thought you wanted me to do something," Jenna said softly, her eyes filled with agony. "I thought you'd be proud of me. That you'd care again."

"I do care. I always cared. Why didn't you talk to me?"

"I tried. You were always so busy with everyone. You looked past me. You gave up on me." Jenna's voice broke and she swallowed hard.

The middle part. It hit Cricket like a slap. That was

the problem. She gave up on the middle part. She'd wanted Jenna to trust her, to learn from her, to be motivated to learn. But the middle part, the work and worry, the little steps, the small failures, the struggle—she'd tried to skip that part.

In everything.

"I'm sorry, Jenna," she said, moving forward. "I let you down. Is it all right if I give you a hug?"

Jenna nodded.

She pulled her into her arms. "I hope you can forgive me."

Jenna nodded against her shoulder.

Cricket heard a sound and looked up to see Tucker in the doorway. He'd obviously heard some of the conversation. "Tucker," she said, and released Jenna. They both turned to look at him.

"The board rejected your resignation," he said.

"They did?"

"I told them everything—where you were that night and how I know. And I asked for a fresh start. For both of us."

"You're kidding," she said, her heart lifting with hope.

"I'm more serious than I've ever been in my life."

"So, you'll stay?" Jenna asked her.

Cricket looked at Jenna for a long moment, saw the hope and trust in her eyes. If Jenna could try again, with all she faced, how could Cricket walk away? She'd thought it was the wise thing to do, but it was actually cowardly. It was quitting when the middle part got muddy.

"Yes, Jenna, I will stay. And I promise we'll work together to get past all this."

Jenna nodded, spilling tears down her cheek. "Okay."

"And I'll want your help when we plan a presentation to Bluestone Development," Cricket said, her throat tight with pride. "And yours, too, Mr. Manning." She looked up at him, her heart swelling with love.

He looked different somehow. There was fire in his eyes, a solidity to his posture that she'd never seen before.

"Can Ms. Wilde and I have a moment?" Tucker asked Jenna.

"Yeah. Sure." Jenna started to leave, then returned for a quick, brusque hug before she left. Cricket would make sure the girl was all right, no matter what. Deciding that, being sure about what she would do, gave her new feelings—peace and confidence.

Tucker shut the door behind Jenna, locked it, and came to Cricket.

"You told them you weren't really married?"

"And that I am in love with you."

"I can't believe you did that. What did Harvey say?"

"He's giving me another chance. A chance to start over here, where I belong. With you." This was the man she'd fallen for in college, full of fire and commitment, true to himself and his beliefs.

"I love you, Cricket. With all my heart. Not because you remind me of how I used to be, but because of how I feel when I'm with you—alive and real and full of hope. Anna was right. I do need a woman with spunk and attitude. Someone who'll give me hell."

"Anna said that?"

"Oh, yeah. Among other things. But she didn't need to tell me that I need your love to feel whole."

"Tucker," she said, hardly able to breathe for how happy she was. Now she had her own doubts to deal with. "I love you, too," she said haltingly. "I guess I'm scared." She studied his face. "What if I don't love you enough?"

He chuckled softly. "It's the middle part, huh?"

She nodded.

"Relax. I'm very good at the middle part." And then he kissed her. It was as glorious and surprising as the first winter kiss, as hot and intense as the stolen embrace in the storage room, and as deep and full of promise as the goodbye lovemaking in her Airstream.

It was solid and tough and full of forever.

"We both get a second chance, Cricket," he said, leaning back to look into her eyes. "I'm going to lighten up and do what Copper Corners High needs, not what I think it needs."

"So you're telling me I was right?"

"About some things. And I'm right about a few things, too. Like that plug over there has too many cords in it." He grinned at her.

"No. Not another fire hazard."

"Who cares?" He shrugged, though she knew tomorrow he'd make her move the cords. "How about we start a whole new fire?"

"But we're at school," she teased. "Isn't that improper?"

"The door's locked and the only living witness is covered in scales and has a brain the size of a thumbtack."

"Mmm. That sounds like the Tucker I kissed under the mistletoe."

"You know, I don't think I ever saw any mistletoe."

"It was in our hearts."

"Yeah." He paused, then said, "We'll take it day by day. You'll love the middle part."

That was the trick to it, she realized—loving the struggle, the work, the step-by-step growth. Learning to manage a chemistry lab, how to let students debate without getting out of control, how to love day by day, a kiss at a time.

"Okay," she said. She reached down to slip her hand in his. The clicking sound made her look down at the wedding band he still wore. "Uh-oh," she teased. "What will your wife say about all this?"

"How many ways can you say 'I told you so'?" He pulled the ring from his finger, then held up the shiny band. "Maybe we can use this. When we're ready for the best part."

"Absolutely." Cricket smiled, not scared at all. In fact, she couldn't wait to see what kind of Jell O Mrs. Thompson would make for the reception.